M000198844

SIRENS

SIRENS

BRADEN CAWTHON

Scholastic Inc.

If you purchased this book without a cover, you should be aware that this book is stolen property. It was reported as "unsold and destroyed" to the publisher, and neither the author nor the publisher has received any payment for this "stripped book."

Copyright © 2023 by Braden Cawthon.

All rights reserved. Published by Scholastic Inc., *Publishers since 1920.* SCHOLASTIC and associated logos are trademarks and/or registered trademarks of Scholastic Inc.

The publisher does not have any control over and does not assume any responsibility for author or third-party websites or their content.

No part of this publication may be reproduced, stored in a retrieval system, or transmitted in any form or by any means, electronic, mechanical, photocopying, recording, or otherwise, without written permission of the publisher. For information regarding permission, write to Scholastic Inc., Attention: Permissions Department, 557 Broadway, New York, NY 10012.

This book is a work of fiction. Names, characters, places, and incidents are either the product of the author's imagination or are used fictitiously, and any resemblance to actual persons, living or dead, business establishments, events, or locales is entirely coincidental.

ISBN 978-1-338-89197-3

10 9 8 7 6 5 4 3 2 1   23 24 25 26 27

Printed in the U.S.A.   40

First printing 2023

Book design by Martha Maynard
Photo © Shutterstock.com

This book is dedicated to my mom, who read every chapter as I wrote it and gave me all of her thoughts, notes, and support to continue writing; my brother, who proofread every chapter for me; and my dad, who motivated me to begin writing and helped get me this opportunity. I can't tell you how much it all means to me.

CHAPTER ONE

Sunlight streamed in through the windows, bathing the room in the warm orange glow of the evening. The TV was buzzing softly with sounds that fell on Joel's inattentive ears—he was half asleep on the couch, eyes closed, watching his little sister Ava's favorite cartoon with her. She was sitting next to him, leaning on his arm, absorbed by the chaotic happenings of the show.

Joel had arrived for the weekend visit about an hour ago, and a dull pain of a headache was beginning to creep into his head from the long drive. He had moved out for college a few months ago, but he returned to visit nearly every weekend to see Ava.

"Hey, you two get ready to go."

His mom's voice snapped through Joel's mind, dragging him back into lucidity. He opened his eyes and, turning his head back, blearily replied, "Go where?"

His mom was bustling about in the room behind them, grabbing various things and stuffing them into her purse. She looked toward Joel for a moment and curtly responded, "We're going out to see a movie, remember?"

Ava, upon hearing this, broke her fixation on the cartoon and, bouncing up from the couch with glee, grabbed Joel's hand and began tugging on it, saying, "Yeah, we're going to see a movie together! You can sit next to me!"

Joel turned back and smiled at Ava before rubbing his eyes for a moment and sighing. "Mom, I'm not feeling up for it right now."

Ava continued tugging on his hand, pouting at him. Joel turned back to face his mom, who returned his gaze with pursed lips. After several moments she sighed, quietly saying, "Ava really wants you to go, Joel."

Ava enthusiastically nodded in agreement, tugging on his hand again and chirping, "Yeah, please, Joey! It's gonna be a really good movie, I promise."

Joel was silent for a moment before sighing again. "Mom, I'm not going to be able to enjoy anything if I have a headache the entire time. You both go ahead; I'll be here all weekend. I just need some time to . . . recuperate."

His mom stared at him for a few moments and then, with an almost inaudible scoff, said, "OK, fine. I hope you feel better when we get back. Ava, go get your shoes; we have to head out soon if we want to get there on time."

Ava's hands dropped and, as Joel turned back around to face her, she jumped up and hugged him, saying, "Come on, please?"

Joel hugged her back, saying, "Hey, I'm just not feeling good right now. You can tell me all about it when you get back, OK? And then we can watch it together here sometime."

Ava sniffled but nodded her head and, mumbling into his shirt, said, "OK . . . I hope you feel better."

"Ava! Shoes, now. We've got to get going."

Their mom's voice snapped through the air again, prompting Ava to bounce up and frantically run around, looking for her shoes. Joel closed his eyes, his head now throbbing with pain. After a minute of listening to the shuffling movements of his mom and Ava, he heard his mom call out, "All right, we'll be back later tonight. There is food in the fridge if you get hungry. Ava, say bye to Joey."

Joel opened his eyes and gave a half-hearted thumbs-up in response. His mom opened the creaky door, her hand on Ava's back. Ava, smiling back at him, called out, "Bye! Love you!"

His mom guided her through the door. Joel smiled at Ava and, waving, quietly called out, "Have fun! Love you too."

The door firmly closed behind them, leaving Joel alone in the empty house. He heard gravel crunching outside before the car engine roared to life. The car was briefly visible through one of the windows as it backed out of the unpaved driveway onto the country road. Ava's face was pressed to the window, waving enthusiastically toward the house. Joel wasn't sure if she could still see him, but he waved back.

Joel sat for several minutes in silence before reaching for his phone in his pocket. As his hand went down, it collided with a soft object lying on the couch. He picked it up—it was a small stuffed kitten toy. Ava usually brought it everywhere she went, lovingly referring to it as "Kitty." He hoped she wouldn't miss it too much while they were out. He continued pulling out his phone and checked the screen.

6:08 p.m.

Notifications: 0

Joel sighed, rubbing his head. *I have classwork I need to do, but I won't be able to get anything done like this anyway. Maybe I should just go lie down and try to sleep off this headache.*

He slowly stood, grimacing slightly, before turning the TV off and shuffling through the empty house toward his room. He stopped by the bathroom momentarily and blearily stared at his own reflection. He was tall, physically fit from regularly working out in high school. His hair wasn't out of control yet, but it was clear that he had let it get away from him after moving out for college, as the wavy brown hair crept toward his ears and down his neck. He reached a hand up and ran it across his face, still mostly smooth since the last time he had shaved. He leaned forward and turned on the faucet, using both hands to splash some water on his face.

He sighed and turned to rummage through the medicine cabinet, grabbing a couple of sleep-aid supplements before making his way to his room. He softly shut the door behind him and sat down on the edge of his bed.

His laptop was still open on the desk in the corner of the room, academic responsibilities beckoning, but Joel was determined to ignore them for now. Joel broke into the small packets and quickly downed the sleeping pills. He stood and, walking over to the desk, firmly closed his laptop. He took his phone out of his pocket again and, turning it to silent mode, plugged it in to charge.

His room, despite the lights being off, was ambiently lit by the orange glow coming from the window. He shuffled over to it and, firmly pulling the blinds closed, plunged his room into near total darkness except for small lines of light escaping through the cracks in the blinds.

Joel collapsed onto his bed and, gently pulling the blankets over himself to combat the chill of the late-autumn air, embraced the relief the darkness provided his eyes. After lying in discomfort for longer than he could keep track of, he slipped into sleep.

———

Joel jumped awake, drenched in a cold sweat. He didn't know what time it was, but the orange sunlight that had slipped through the blinds had now been replaced by the brilliant silvery-white glow of moonlight.

All was silent and still around him. Catching his breath, he threw the blankets off and sat up. His head was still foggy, but a sense of unease penetrated through his mind. Swinging his legs off the side of the bed, he stood, taking a cursory glance around his room—all seemed normal.

Joel walked to the window and, splitting the blinds with two fingers, looked outside across the dimly lit plains—there wasn't any movement except for the grass gently rolling in the breeze and the branches of the occasional tree swaying. He frowned, as if he somehow hoped his discomfort would be validated, before he firmly closed the blinds and, after a moment of agitation, made his way back into the living room.

Outside the confines of his room, his mind seemed to clear. After briefly scanning the room, Joel sighed and walked to the front door. Opening it, he stepped outside onto the porch, which was basked in shadow from the overhang.

The moon was hidden behind the cover of clouds, though there was still enough ambient light to see. Nothing disturbed the silence, nor broke the regularity of the breeze. The horizon was still very dimly glowing with the vibrant colors of the sunset, though the sun itself had vanished.

It can't be that late if the sun just set, then. Ava and Mom should be on their way home by now. After pondering for a moment, attempting to calculate how long it would take to drive to the city and back, he shook his head and dispelled the thought.

A sense of unease crept down his spine again as he looked out onto the moonlit plains. He frowned, quickly turning around and going back inside. He made his way back to his bedroom, now in complete darkness as his eyes attempted to readjust, and lay back down on the bed. As time passed, the lingering effects of the sleeping pills helped ease his restlessness and lower him into a fretful sleep.

By the time Joel finally woke, his room was shining with bright afternoon sun streaming in through the cracks in the blinds. He groaned, feeling stiff from the very long night of sleep. *Maybe I shouldn't have taken two of those pills . . . I'm surprised Ava hasn't woken me up yet.* He reached for his phone to check the time, only to realize he left it plugged in on the desk across the room.

Swearing to himself, he forced himself out of bed and shambled over to the desk and sat down. Unplugging his phone, the screen turned on.

12:47 p.m.

Notifications: 20

Mom—Missed Call: 14

New Voicemails: 5

Emergency Alert: 1

Joel's eyes widened for a moment in shock, but he quickly regained his composure and, frantically tapping through the notifications, began listening to the voicemails.

11:33 p.m. "Hey, Joel, we might be late getting home tonight. There is some sort of storm blowing in, and sirens are going off all over the city. Ava and I are still at the movie theater; we got ushered into one of the auditoriums, away from the windows."

11:35 p.m. "The alarms are getting louder—I don't know what's going on. I can't see what's going on outside in this theater, but maybe that's for the best. Ava is scared, but I think we'll be OK. Could you call me and talk to her? You're really good with her; she would feel a lot better. Call please."

Joel could distinctly hear the high-pitched whine of what sounded like a tornado siren in the background of the message. His mom's voice had carried a small amount of panic in the first two messages, but in the next ones he could tell that she was on the brink of a breakdown.

11:54 p.m. "Hey, we're going to be stuck here for the night, I don't think this is going to blow over. Stay safe over there, OK? I don't know what it's like over there, but stay inside."

11:56 p.m. "Joel, don't come into the city. Whatever you do, stay out there, please. I'll bring Ava back safe, we'll come back tomorrow when this is all over. But please, stay home. Don't—"

The voicemail abruptly cut off mid-sentence. Joel quickly tapped on the last voicemail, which was marked as having been made almost two hours after the last, but heard nothing except for the unrelenting wail of the emergency alarms. He turned the volume up and pressed his phone to his ear, but still heard nothing other than the sirens.

He stood, looking at his phone in disbelief, his hands shaking. The only notification on his screen now was the emergency warning, which read:

Emergency Alert: 11:25 p.m. Severe weather alert in this area until further notice. Take shelter. Check local media for updates.

He shook his head, shutting out all thoughts for a moment,

and attempted to call his mom—to no avail. He tried to call a couple more times before letting out a strained yell of frustration. He closed his eyes and exhaled slowly, willing himself to calm down, before opening his eyes and checking his phone again, only to this time notice that he had no signal whatsoever. He scoffed and put his phone in his pocket, then stood still in his room for a few moments, his mind reeling. Joel quickly made his way out of his room to the TV, and turned it on, flipping through the channels to find the news.

His eyes darted back and forth across the lit screen as he clicked back through the channel's history—only to find that there were no broadcasts at all from the area since last night. Joel was overwhelmed for a second, and braced himself against the wall. *What the hell is going on up there?*

His panic passed in a moment, replaced with a steely determination. *It's already midday and they aren't back yet—I need to go find them. Mom might have stayed at that theater if she couldn't drive out with Ava, so that's where I need to head.* He quickly made a lap around the house, grabbing some necessities—a couple bottles of water, a flashlight, and some food—before swiftly making his way outside into the afternoon sun. He threw his supplies into the back seat before climbing into his car and beginning the long ride north to the city.

Joel's mind was chaotic as he drove, pushing his car as fast as he could. *What could possibly have been going on last night?* He couldn't conceive of any disaster that made sense. *It can't have been a tornado—there hasn't been a storm like that here in a decade, and there wasn't even a damn cloud in the sky yesterday.*

He shook his head, attempting to clear his mind. No matter what happened, he needed to make sure Ava and his mom were safe. And so, he continued driving, soaring down the lone country roads, stuck with nothing but his own thoughts and anxieties.

As time went by and he got closer to the more urbanized areas around the city, something else began nagging him— he had not seen a single car driving the opposite way. He had brushed it off before, as typically the farther out into the country he went, the less traffic there was in any direction, but by now there surely would be some, especially if there had been some monumental disaster. He pushed the questions aside again, trying to focus solely on getting to the city.

Eventually he saw the outskirts of the suburbs ahead of him. And with it, he saw a car in the opposite lane of the road. He sighed, relieved by the sight—until he went soaring past it. The car wasn't moving at all, and there was no one inside it. He barely had a moment to think about this before looking back up and seeing a car stalled in his lane.

Adrenaline spiked through Joel as he slammed on the brakes, yanking the wheel to the right and veering off the road onto the shoulder. His car came to a screeching halt.

Joel's knuckles were white in a deadlock grip on the wheel, shaken by the very near full-speed collision. He breathed heavily for a few moments, not releasing his hold on the wheel, before finally calming down enough to act. He opened his door and stepped out, walking to the middle of the road before peering as far as he could see in either direction. There were more stalled cars for several miles ahead of him, some in either lane, some on the shoulder, and some even entirely out on the grass on either side of the road.

There wasn't a person in sight. *It looks like people tried to leave the city, but then just . . . abandoned their cars in the road.* After a moment of transfixion, he hesitantly walked back to his car and, scouting the road ahead of him, began slowly weaving between stalled cars. It was approaching evening now, the sun well on its way toward the horizon.

As Joel got closer to the suburbs, the streets were increasingly cluttered with wrecks—some were crashed into street lamps, others completely overturned in ditches, and still others smoking and stuck together from head-on collisions.

Eventually, Joel reached a point where the density of the cars and wreckage in his path made him unable to continue driving. He came to an apprehensive halt, parking his car along with the rest of them.

He was well within the suburbs now, and yet he still had not seen a single person. All the houses within his view were either shut, their windows covered, or even more disturbingly, left with their front doors open. Joel grabbed his few supplies from the back seat of his car before reluctantly locking it and leaving it there. *I'm going to be moving at a snail's pace on foot, but I don't have much of an option right now.*

He began walking down the street, the skyscrapers of the city center looming in the distance, though with his ability to drive stripped from him, they were now seemingly out of reach. Despite this, he continued walking with steely determination, weaving through all the obstacles in the road.

He had no clue how long he had been walking, but the sun was dipping closer to the horizon by the minute. He frowned—he wasn't particularly inclined to try to traverse miles of suburban area on foot at night, especially given how little he knew of the situation. As he stood there considering his options, his flow of thought was interrupted by a shriek.

"What're you doing?!"

Before his mind had even processed that another human

yelled this, something slammed into him from the side and began pushing him off the road toward one of the houses. "Get the hell off me!" Joel shouted, stepping to the side and pushing back at the unknown person. They stepped back, and Joel had a moment to look at whoever this person who rammed into him was. It was a tall woman, olive skinned with short, raven-black hair and a fierce look in her eyes. She appeared just a few years older than him and carried herself with confidence.

She raised her eyebrows at him in bewilderment before approaching him again, saying in a strained but measured voice, "Saving your life. I think. Come with me." She grabbed his arm and yanked him forward, pulling him toward a house with an open door.

Joel opened his mouth to object to her dragging him along, but after a moment he decided against it. *Even if she seems a bit crazy, maybe she knows what's going on.* Upon entering the house, she slammed the door behind them. Before Joel could even get a word out, she ran off into a different room of the house.

Joel followed her, unsure of what to make of her behavior. He caught a glimpse of her shutting the blinds in the room ahead of him before she darted off into a different room. Joel sighed, and then simply resigned himself to wait by the door until she came back to explain herself. *Does she even live here? How did she know that there was nobody already here?* Before Joel could let these thoughts develop, she popped back into view in the room in front of him.

"This house has a basement; we can stay here. Come in here, away from the door. Do you have any idea how much I risked going out there to save your ass?"

Joel stammered as he walked into the room, unable to answer for a moment, before regaining composure and responding, "No, I was hoping you could explain. My mom and my little sister came into the city last night, and I got a lot of . . . disturbing voicemails from them last night. I came here to come find them and make sure they are OK, but I can't even get there because of all the road blockage."

The woman considered this for a moment, tapping her foot rhythmically against the wood floor, before responding, "You weren't here last night? You don't know what's going on?"

Joel raised an eyebrow, saying, "Yeah, that was the implication. I assume you were here, though?"

The woman frowned before sighing and replying, talking very quickly.

"I can try to catch you up, but I don't even know where to begin. I don't know what's happening *exactly*, but I know

15

enough to know that being outside right now is a very bad idea. It started last night, sometime after sunset. I think the power grid went down, because everything in my house turned off, and all the lights in the neighborhood turned off too. Then I heard a tornado siren, coming from somewhere downtown. It started as just one, then I think more of them started going off because it got louder. A bit after that is when the emergency alert went out about staying indoors, so I did. I was watching from the window of my room, though—there were people walking around, looking confused and restless. Some were talking to each other; others were making their way back to their houses. Lots of people got in their cars and started to drive away. The sounds of the alarms started getting closer—louder and louder as the night went on. They just kept getting louder. The longer I sat there watching, the more disturbed my head was. I felt like I couldn't think properly. And then . . . I . . ."

She stuttered, staring blankly at the floor, eyes wide open. After a moment she snapped out of it, shaking her head before apprehensively continuing her story.

"A siren started to go off in our neighborhood. I can't describe it. It sounded like it was coming from directly above us; it wasn't normal. It just kept going, and going—it never stopped. I got away from my window and tried to get as far away from the sound as possible, plugging my ears with head-phones and covering them. I don't even know how long I was there, but at some point, all the sound suddenly stopped. Every alarm turned off. I got up and made my way back to the window and took one look outside—I could see the sky just starting to get bright on the horizon as the sun was fix-ing to come up. But then, I saw someone who was still in the street, writhing on the ground and looking up into the sky. Then the sun came up, and they . . . stopped moving."

She stopped again, seemingly frozen in recollection. After a moment of stunned silence, Joel cleared his throat and quietly asked:

"What . . . What happened to the person in the street? I didn't see anyone at all on my drive here, anywhere. No one in the streets, no one in any of the cars stalled in the road, no one in the houses. You're the only person I've seen."

She looked up at him again, and after a brief pause, said very slowly, seemingly choosing her words carefully.

"They were gone when I looked again later. I don't know what happened or where they went, but they're gone."

She looked down at her wrist, at an old-fashioned watch. She closed her eyes for a moment and let out a long, anxious breath before looking back up at him, and whispered:

"It's almost sunset. We need to get into the basement, now."

She sprung up and began marching out of the room, before stopping for a moment in consideration. She walked back and grabbed a chair, then placed it firmly in front of the front door, blocking the handle. When she was satisfied with the placement, she walked out of sight again and called out, "Come on! Basement, now."

Joel sat still for a moment, his mind reeling from her grotesque story. *How much of that can possibly be true?* He bit his lip in indecision, thinking, before wordlessly getting up and following her, giving the front door one panicked look before slowly descending the steps.

Joel closed the door behind him as he entered the basement. It was cramped and sparse, with nothing but a shelf with an assortment of old tools and a single light fixture hanging from the ceiling, which was burning dimly. The woman was rummaging through the items on the shelf, muttering to herself. Joel watched her for a moment, confused, before prodding.

"What're you doing?"

"Looking for something to plug our ears with."

"I . . . We're underground, why is that—"

She cut him off with a glare.

"Just in case. I don't know how loud it's going to be down here. Do you have a light?"

18

Joel reached into his bag, rummaging around for a moment before finding his flashlight and presenting it to her.

"Good, we might need it. I'm not sure if it was related, but when it started last night, the power went out."

She let out an exasperated sigh and gave up her search. She walked to one of the walls and, putting her back against it, slid down into a seated position. She looked up at Joel, clearly very anxious about their situation, and muttered, "So, what's your name? We are going to be here for a while, might as well get to know each other."

She looked down at her watch again, then up at the small light on the ceiling. Joel considered her behavior for a moment before responding.

"Joel. You?"

"Emily. Nice to meet you, despite the circumstances."

Joel, following her example, sat by the wall opposite of Emily.

"So, have you seen or heard from anyone who was living downtown since last night?"

He asked this with a vain hope, knowing there most likely wouldn't be. Emily bit her lip and shook her head apologetically, quietly saying, "No, not a peep. I . . . I think that if anyone farther into the city stayed put like I did and didn't go outside, they'll be fine for now."

Both of them fell silent. The minutes ticked by, with Emily getting increasingly agitated. Joel eventually broke the silence.

"So . . . do you have any family in the city? I am going farther in tomorrow, no matter how dangerous it is. If you were heading that way too, we could . . ." Joel's statement petered off, but the question hung in the air.

"No, but going *out* of the city is suicide. The roads are blocked so we would be going by foot, and it would be nightfall again by the time we made it anywhere. I am not taking a risk hoping that whatever is happening is only within the city. So . . . I'll figure what my plan is tomorrow."

Despite her not answering his proposition, Joel moved on.

"Well, we don't even know if it will happen again. All we know is that *something* went down last night, but . . ."

The light above them flickered, then turned off.

They were in complete darkness and silence. Joel's words got caught in his throat. He fumbled with his flashlight before turning it on, propping it up against a wall to provide a small source of light in the room. Emily spoke up, quietly muttering, "We are safe down here. Just block out the sounds. We are safe down here as long as we don't go outside." Joel wasn't sure if she was talking to him, or herself.

"How did you make it through last night? Were you in a

basement, or . . . ?" Joel let his question hang, unsure of what exactly he was asking.

"No, but luckily I had something to plug my ears with right away. I don't know what it will be like without that."

Several more minutes passed in silence. Joel could hear Emily's breathing getting quicker. From what little he could see of her in the dim, narrow range of light provided by the flashlight, she was huddled against the wall, her arms firmly hugging her legs against her.

As the seconds ticked by, Joel felt a sense of unease spreading through him, like his feeling from the night before. He didn't hear anything yet, but something felt . . . *off*.

It has to be well past sunset by now. Maybe whatever happened last night isn't going to happen again. Am I just sitting in this basement for no reason when I could be out there crossing more ground? Very soon after those thoughts passed through his head, he heard a distinct whine. It was very faint, but present. Joel was about to speak up, but Emily beat him to it.

"There's the first alarm. Probably in the city center. More of them are going to start going off."

"Why wouldn't the officials make some sort of statement warning people if they knew it was going to start again? Why just set off all the alarms and freak people out even more?"

"I don't know. Whatever the case, there has to be a reason

21

for them all being set off, and I know that we can't go outside. We are safe if we stay inside. We just have to stomach the noise."

As she was saying this, Joel heard another siren go off in the distance—still faint, but this one was perhaps closer than the last. Then another. The sound was compounding quickly—every few seconds a new one overlapped, making a distant wall of white noise in the background. It was getting louder, and closer.

Joel's stomach twisted into a knot as the sounds increased, his mind feeling hazy and muddled.

"So what's our plan? Are we just going to sit here for the entire night? Couldn't we—"

Emily cut him off mid-sentence, sharply saying, "Yes, our plan is just to sit here until the sun comes up. If you want any chance of finding your family, the night is not an option."

Joel didn't respond—the blaring sirens were getting loud enough to be disruptive to conversation at this point, despite them being underground. Then, abruptly, the noises got significantly more piercing—it sounded like they had started to go off in the neighborhood itself. He began to say something to Emily, but quickly realized there was no way she would be able to tell what he was saying.

He covered his ears, putting his head down on his knees, and tried to wait it out. The noise was unrelenting, unwavering—somehow it seemed to get louder as time went on, despite the ones in the neighborhood already going off. It felt like the sounds were crawling their way into his head, sabotaging his thoughts. He didn't know how long he had been sitting there, but eventually he felt his consciousness fading, and he slipped into darkness.

CHAPTER TWO

I stepped back. Each heartbeat rang in my ears like a drum.

One. I dropped what I held.

Two. I looked at the blood on my hands.

Three. My vision blurred from tears.

Four. Five. Six.

Nothing.

Joel slowly opened his eyes. The light above him was shining again, and the door up to the ground floor was hanging open. The flashlight still sat beside him, the battery now drained, and Emily was no longer with him in the room. He pushed himself off the ground, and immediately winced— he had a splitting headache, and his ears were still throbbing from the torrent of abuse last night. He gathered himself for a moment before slowly standing up and making his way upstairs.

Bright morning light was streaming in through the cracks

in the blinds, and the house was completely silent except for the creaking of wood from someone walking on the second floor, which he assumed was Emily. He approached the window in front of him and, cracking the blinds with two fingers, peered outside. Everything was the same as the previous evening—cars stalled in the road, doors opened in random houses, and not a person in sight.

He closed the blinds again and wandered around the house, looking for stairs to go to the second floor. He passed through the living room they were in the night before, but this time he stopped and looked around. There were mementos of various sorts on shelves, pictures on the walls. He approached one of the pictures and, picking it up, observed it: It was a family portrait, with two parents and their son. Joel felt a small lump in his throat, and put it back down.

He quickly found the stairs, and went up. It was a rather cramped floor, all things considered—it seemed that the upstairs was dedicated only to bedrooms. To his right was what he assumed was the master bedroom, and to his left were two other bedrooms. The door of one of the rooms to the left was closed, and the other was open slightly—through it, he could see a shadow moving about. He walked to the ajar door and opened it fully, revealing a small bedroom where

Emily was sitting by the window, peering outside with binoculars. At the sound of him opening the door, Emily jumped and, turning around, exclaimed, "Knock, would you? Just about scared the life out of me."

Joel, embarrassed, stammered for a moment before quietly muttering, "Yeah, sorry . . . Who else would be here, anyway?"

Emily shook her head and returned her gaze to the window. Joel looked around the room. It was clearly a child's room—there were toys scattered about on the floor and in a large bin, and there were drawings taped above the bedframe. Pushing the observation out of his head, he walked over to Emily and, peering through the window too, inquired, "Did you make it all right through the night?"

Emily looked back at him again, a troubled expression on her face.

"No. I think I passed out at some point. It was worse than the first night. Let's hope that it doesn't keep getting worse."

Joel nodded in agreement, and Emily began peering out the window again. Joel peered up at the sky—it looked to be well past noon already. *I was out for a long time.*

"What are you looking at?"

"I have a decent view into the downtown area with these binoculars, but I'm not learning much. There is no activity on the roads, but I'm watching because I saw a group of people earlier. I'm seeing if there are more or if it was just them."

Joel was taken aback for a second, before exclaiming, "You *saw people*? Where? What were they doing?"

"It wasn't too far from here, maybe a couple of miles down. I saw three people walking down the highway, farther into the city, carrying bags of something."

Joel barely had a chance to respond before Emily stood up and packed the binoculars into her bag. She continued, "If there are other survivors at all, there might be a larger group of people. They might know what's going on. In any case, the water *also* stopped working as of last night, so I can't stay here. I might as well go with you to try to find other people and figure out what's going on."

Joel, considering the proposition, was apprehensive. *The situation could also get worse, but she's right. I'm planning on going into the city anyway—but I wasn't planning on trying to find anyone other than Ava and Mom, though.* Joel hesitantly responded, "OK. Let's do it." Emily nodded and briskly walked out of the room.

Joel heard her quick steps down the flight of stairs followed by her voice calling out behind her, "Pack up your stuff, and let's head out. I'll grab any food I can find." Joel, still conflicted about the situation, slowly began following her. He stopped, though, in front of the other bedroom with the closed door. He reached out and slowly opened the door, peering inside. It was mostly empty, with sealed boxes lying around the ground, with one exception—there was a half-assembled crib in the corner of the room.

Joel clenched his teeth and shut the door before following Emily downstairs. She was darting around, checking different drawers and cabinets—presumably looking for supplies of any kind. Joel snatched his bag and joined Emily in pillaging the house for anything useful. He grabbed as many bottles of water as he could and a small pack of batteries for his flashlight, then replaced the drained ones.

Joel called out, "All right, I'm ready."

"OK, give me a second. I am just going to go check something really quick."

Emily popped back into view, walking through the room, before disappearing around the corner. Joel heard her footsteps going back up the stairs. He followed her, curious, and upon reaching the top of the stairs found that the master bedroom's door was ajar. He walked over and, knocking first this time, opened the door. Emily was checking the drawers in the room. Joel, one eyebrow raised questioningly, asked, "What are you looking for?"

"Earplugs for sleeping—it would help block out the sound during the night. Help me look." Joel, nodding in acknowledgment, made his way to the closet in the back of the room. Opening it and looking inside, he found there wasn't much to see. There was an assortment of clothes and boxes filled with blankets and sheets, and what looked like a couple of toolboxes up on one of the shelves in the corner.

Joel reached for those boxes and, one by one, began opening them and inspecting what they contained. The first had a screwdriver and drill bits, the second had an assortment of cables, and . . . Joel stopped for a moment when he opened the third, looking down at a small handgun and a case of ammunition. He took both out of the case and shut it, and, walking back into the master bedroom, called out to Emily:

"Hey, uh, I found this. Do you think we should . . . ?" Joel let the question hang, presenting the gun. Emily turned around, looking up at Joel for a second before seeing what he was holding. She considered it for a moment before saying, "Yeah, bring it with you. Never know what we might need."

Joel nodded and asked, "Did you find any earplugs?"

Emily shook her head in frustration. Joel frowned, responding, "Oh. Well . . . If we can find a convenience store along the road, maybe they might have some. If we can, uh . . . get in."

Emily, eyebrow raised at his hesitant words, shrugged in response. Looking back at the drawers one last time, she murmured, "Yeah, I guess. All right, let's go." Joel nodded in acknowledgment before heading back downstairs. He stashed the gun and ammo in his bag before hoisting it over his shoulder and making his way to the front door.

The chair that Emily had propped against the door last night was still there, firmly pressed up against the door handle. As Joel dislodged it, Emily joined him in the foyer, now laden with a backpack. Joel reached out and, grabbing the handle, looked back at Emily, who nodded and gestured toward the door. Joel turned back and, twisting the handle, led them out into the blinding afternoon sun.

After his eyes adjusted to the light, Joel gave a cursory look at their surroundings. Despite the chaos of last night, all was exactly the same as it was. Emily, squinting and covering her eyes, looked toward the sun, and then at her watch.

"We have somewhere around seven hours of daylight left, and the downtown area is almost thirty miles away. We had better get moving."

Emily walked toward the road, Joel following close

behind. They both began making their way through the empty, lifeless suburbs toward the city center.

"God, my feet hurt. How long have we been walking?"

The sun was significantly lower in the sky now. They hadn't encountered the people Emily had spotted earlier, nor had they seen anything unusual except the roads littered with stalled vehicles. The towering high-rises of the city center were significantly closer but too far away to reach before nightfall. Emily looked at her watch, then up into the sky before responding.

"Around six hours. We should probably find a place to stay the night. We don't want to end up stuck outside when the sun goes down."

Joel agreed, and they continued walking.

"There, that'll work." When Emily stopped as she said this, Joel almost ran into her, his mind in a daze of worry and stress. She was pointing at what looked like a gas station, a long way down the road to their right. *I wouldn't have spotted that—but, I guess I haven't really been looking either.* Emily peered back at him, head tilted. "What do you think?"

"Yeah, there might be useful supplies there as well. Let's go."

They parted from the highway they had been walking on and, after a short while, entered the parking lot of the gas station. Much like everything else they had come across so far, there was no life to be seen. There were cars abandoned at the pumps, some with the hoses still in, others stalled halfway out of the lot.

One hose was hanging drearily from the pump, with a puddle of gasoline beneath it. The lights were off in the building, and the doors were closed. The entire front face of the store was made of glass, with ads plastered intermittently across them. Joel, taking stock of the situation, asked Emily, "Well, should we go try the door? Doesn't seem like anyone is home."

"Yeah, but if it's locked, let's just stay somewhere else. We have enough time to go find another place. I can't imagine it would be locked, though."

They walked to the door and, as Emily suspected, they were able to manually slide it open with ease. The interior was relatively small, with one row of refrigerated shelves with drinks and a couple aisles of various snacks and needs. There looked to be a bathroom in the back, as well as a stockroom that was helpfully labeled EMPLOYEES ONLY.

Emily quickly walked forward and, while rummaging through the shelves, called out to Joel, "Restock with whatever you need while we are here, and look for those earplugs." Joel nodded and made his way to the drinks, looking for bottled water. As he scanned the first shelf, he was interrupted.

"H-hey! Who are you?"

Joel spun around toward the voice, and saw Emily do the same, instinctively stepping back from it. A skinny, shaggy-haired teenager, just a few years younger than Joel, stood in the doorway of the employees-only room, holding a box cutter out in front of him with one hand. His hands were filthy, and his blond hair was matted with dirt. He was wearing a branded name tag, with the faded name JEREMY scrawled on it with permanent marker. His hand was shaking profusely, and his eyes were darting back and forth between the two of them. Joel held up his hands as he slowly replied, "Easy—my name is Joel, that's Emily. We're just here for shelter for the night—I assume that's why you're here too?"

Jeremy didn't respond for a few moments, still frantically scanning both of them, before he slowly lowered the box cutter.

"Yeah. I was working the night shift when it started. I was in the back unloading a pallet. I just stayed back there for the whole night. I . . ." He cut himself off, firmly closing his mouth and raising the box cutter again slightly. Emily, seeing this, spoke up again.

"Well, if you made it through two nights back there, we would really appreciate it if you let us stay the night here too, then we will be on our way. We are heading to the city center, but we can't travel at night."

The three of them stood in silence, the tension palpable in the air. After a few moments, Jeremy sighed and, sliding the blade into the metal sheath, put the box cutter in his pocket. He quietly muttered, "Yeah, you can stay. Take whatever you need tonight, but tomorrow I want you gone. I need to make this stuff last until all this blows over."

Joel exhaled in relief, but Emily remained tense, not moving an inch. Joel responded, "Thank you, we appreciate it. There doesn't happen to be any earplugs here, are there? To block the sound." He gestured toward his ears as he said this, raising an eyebrow.

Jeremy stood still for a moment, his hands shaking slightly, before quietly walking to one of the shelves and grabbing two items. He then walked over to Joel, showing him the packets, which read NIGHTTIME EARPLUGS FOR BETTER SLEEPING. *Perfect.*

"Thank you. This will help us a lot." Joel reached out as he said this and grabbed the two packets, but Jeremy didn't let go of them. Joel looked up at him in confusion. Jeremy was just staring at him blankly, one eye twitching. Joel looked at Emily, who was watching the interaction. She began slowly creeping toward them. Before Emily got too close though, Jeremy released the earplugs, his expression returning to normal.

"Sure. If you need anything else, let me know."

He turned around and walked back to the stockroom. Just before he disappeared into the back, he called, "Just make sure you are back here before nightfall. Glass doesn't do much to help." Joel looked toward the front of the store as he said this. He could see a good amount of sunlight through the glass still. He looked at Emily, who just shrugged in response. She walked over toward him and, as he began prying open the packaging around the earplugs, quietly asked, "What do you make of that? Dude was acting weird."

Joel looked up at her. She looked concerned, biting her lip.

"I don't know. He is probably just stressed out of his mind. Some high schooler stuck holed up in a gas station, having survived the past two nights completely alone in the back room, not able to leave to find his folks."

"Yeah, but still, I think we should just get our supplies and go; we have some time to find another shelter for the night."

Joel pondered for a moment, eyebrows furrowed.

"If there is any risk of us getting caught outside, we shouldn't take it. At this point, I think our best move is to just wait it out here. We have shelter and supplies. This will give us some more time to think about our strategy once we get into the city too."

Joel handed one of the pairs of earplugs to her. She grabbed them and, while inspecting them, responded, "Fine. I guess there is a lot of food and water here, but I still don't trust the guy. We just need to keep our eye on him in case he acts . . . irrationally." Joel agreed, putting his earplugs in his pocket. They returned to collecting what they needed, before heading back to the stockroom.

It was a rather cramped space, but it spanned the width of the building. There was another door at the far end of the stockroom that led outside, but boxes had been pushed in front of it and a large piece of cardboard was haphazardly attached over the window with packing tape. The space was dimly lit overhead with old fluorescent lights, some of which weren't working. Jeremy sat with his back against the far wall, adjacent to the door, staring down the length of the room at them. He didn't acknowledge their entrance—after seeing them, he simply looked down at the floor and mindlessly tapped the ground next to him with his fingers.

Emily and Joel glanced at each other at the sight of this,

and then proceeded to make their way slowly down the room, leaving the door behind them open for the moment. There were shelves lined with various sealed products, as well as a couple pallets stacked high with boxes, all of which had been opened. The floor was littered with pieces of trash—chip bags, empty bottles of water, and other packaging.

"Close the door before the sun goes down. Just sit down anywhere. Gonna be a long night." Jeremy's voice cut through the silence, causing both of them to jump. He was now staring directly ahead at them. As Emily slowly nodded in response, Jeremy returned his gaze to the floor, and resumed the mindless tapping. Emily looked down at her watch, then whispered to Joel, "I'll go sit by the door and watch the time. You just keep an eye on Jeremy."

"How much longer do we have until sundown?"

"Around half an hour. I have a good view of the horizon from here, I'll shut the door when it makes contact."

"All right. I'll just sit here so there is plenty of room between us and him."

Emily nodded, peering back at Jeremy nervously, before walking back toward the front door and leaning against the wall in front of it. Joel slowly sat down, his back against a small stack of boxes, wincing as pain shot up his legs, which were very sore from the long hours of travel. He frowned and reached into his pocket to pull out his phone. He clicked the screen on and squinted at the bright light as he swiped through menus to find his contacts. He attempted to call his mom again, to no avail. He checked his signal—zero bars still, even in the city. He glanced up at Emily and quietly asked, "Is yours working?"

Emily was already looking at him inquisitively, the light from his phone having caught her attention. She shook her head but pulled her own phone out anyway to show him, saying, "No, nothing. Ever since the first night, it's all been dark."

Joel nodded and slowly put his phone back into his pocket, sighing. Several minutes passed in silence, and he soon became lost in his thoughts.

He rubbed his forehead, both tired and anxious about the night to come. *There are barely any people out here. Either everyone closer to the city made it to some sort of refuge, or . . .* Joel felt a lump in his throat before he discarded the thought. *I still don't even know what this is. The alarms are obviously frightening, but we don't know why they are going off, or where everyone disappeared to. We just need to find more people and try to learn as much about this as possible.* As the thought ran through his mind, he glanced at Jeremy, who hadn't moved an inch since their last interaction. Joel cleared his throat before asking, "So, uh, Jeremy, right? Do you know what any of this is about? You were closer to the middle of the city for all of this, so maybe you have some more information or have seen people who know more."

Jeremy looked up at him, a blank expression on his face. "No. I haven't left this building since it started." He gestured at all the trash on the floor as he said this. "I've seen a few people walking by carrying big bags of something, but they didn't come into the building."

Joel considered this for a moment before he made a connection in his mind.

"How many? Was it three people?"

Jeremy nodded, looking agitated. "Yeah, why? Do you know them?"

"No, but we were walking today in the same direction as them, hoping to run into them or other people. We are just trying to figure out what's going on."

Jeremy didn't even respond to the statement—he simply returned his gaze to the floor, apparently done with the conversation. Joel sighed, returning back to his thoughts. Not long after that, Emily's voice cut through his mind.

"All right, the sun just hit the horizon. Lights out."

Emily reached forward and, grabbing the knob, firmly pulled the door shut. After a moment, she called out, "Joel, could you come over here and help me pull one of the shelves in front of the door? It doesn't lock."

"Yeah, one second."

Joel pushed himself up from the floor, grimacing, before making his way over to Emily, who was standing ready next to a small shelving unit. Joel took hold of the other side of it and, after counting down, the two of them shifted the shelf in front of the door. Just as Joel was about to turn around to walk back, Emily grabbed his shoulder and stopped him, whispering, "Stay over here. This might be the safest place for us, but still . . ."

Her eyes darted toward Jeremy before she continued. "Just in case we need to make a quick exit, sit over by the other side of that shelving unit so we can move it out of the way as fast as possible." Joel nodded and, putting his bag down next to Emily's, seated himself on the wall adjacent to her. Jeremy didn't seem to notice that Joel didn't return to where he was seated before.

Emily sat back down as well, reaching into her pockets and pulling out her earplugs, which she pushed into place. She looked at Joel and tapped on them. Emily called out across the room, "Hey, remember to put your plugs in. It should help a lot."

Jeremy didn't respond, but after a moment, he did appear

to reach into his pocket and put something into each of his ears. Joel then retrieved his earplugs from his pockets and pushed them into his ears as firmly as he could, which left him hearing nothing but his breathing and heartbeat.

None of them moved for a few minutes, as they waited for the inevitable. Finally, the fluorescent lights above them flickered a couple of times before buzzing out, leaving them in darkness. After a minute, two bright beams of light appeared—Emily had both Joel's and her flashlight ready from their bags. She handed Joel his, and Joel mouthed a thank-you.

Emily had her flashlight pointed up, providing enough light to vaguely see a few feet around them despite the angle; Joel simply turned his off, in case it was needed later. There was a third, dimmer light from the other side of the room—the first beams of moonlight were creeping in below the door and from the edges of the makeshift cardboard window cover next to Jeremy, which illuminated his hair and legs but left the rest of him in darkness. Several more minutes passed in silence.

Joel's mind began to feel unsettled again—he could almost hear the sounds inside his head, despite them not having started yet. His mind almost felt constricted, making it difficult to think. A few minutes later, he began to feel the vibrations in his head, and could faintly hear the blaring alarms. As opposed to last night, however, this was much more bearable; the earplugs seemed to be working. Emily waved at him, and, attempting to communicate, gave a thumbs-up and shrugged. Joel confirmed her question, giving a thumbs-up in return. Emily nodded, returning her gaze down the room.

The alarms quickly reached their maximum volume, leaving Joel able to hear nothing but a dull buzzing in his head and a faint, high-pitched whine. While more tolerable, it was still grating on his mind. Joel flicked on his flashlight and observed the pallet of boxes on the other side of the room. Now, at eye level with the lower boxes, he saw things that he hadn't seen before.

There were markings and slashes covering the boxes in random patterns. He shifted his flashlight, looking farther down the room—every single box had gashes strewn all over it. He looked at Emily, who was also now squinting at the boxes with concern. She looked just as disturbed as Joel felt. Her eyes darted up at Jeremy, who still hadn't moved. She turned her gaze to Joel and mouthed, "I'll watch him." Joel nodded, turning off his flashlight to conserve the battery. Joel's head began throbbing, the sounds echoing around his head, leaving him unable to think about anything else.

Several more minutes passed before Emily slowly leaned

forward and tapped Joel's hand to get his attention. He quickly looked up at her—her gaze, and flashlight, were fixed down the hall. Turning his head, he peered down the hall as well. Jeremy had stood up, and was bracing with one arm against the door. He wasn't looking at the two of them— he was looking directly at the door. Joel and Emily shared a glance, before the two of them slowly stood up.

Joel squinted at Jeremy, trying to see what was wrong. Emily grabbed Joel's arm again to get his attention, then she tapped her ears. Joel looked back at Jeremy and his eyes widened—he didn't have anything in his ears. Just as he noticed this, Jeremy grabbed the top corner of the cardboard and ripped it off the window, flooding the end of the room with the radiant silvery-white light of the moon. He frantically began shoving the boxes out of the way of the door.

Joel gasped and sprinted down the room, Emily close behind. When he reached Jeremy, he grabbed his shoulders and yanked him back from the door. Jeremy struggled furiously and, when Emily approached, leapt up and kicked her in the stomach, putting all his weight on Joel, causing her to stumble back and double over. As Joel and Jeremy fell backward, he broke free of Joel's grip.

Jeremy's attention turned from the door to him. Now bathed fully in the moonlight, Joel could see him clearly for the first time since the lights went out—he had a frenzied look in eyes, his arms and legs marred by scratches, and his fingernails were stained with blood. Jeremy leapt on top of Joel and, grabbing either side of his head, ripped his ear-plugs out.

Joel was dazed for a moment by the intensity of the sirens. The noise filled his head, pushing out all other thoughts, incapacitating him. Jeremy put his hand around Joel's throat and squeezed—Joel couldn't even resist. In the back of his consciousness, he recognized that Jeremy was screaming something, somehow making himself heard over the sirens.

"They . . . They WHISPER to me; I can't get them out of my head! Never-ending, ceaseless words, speaking directly into my soul!"

Jeremy let go of Joel's neck and then grabbed his own head, gripping his hair so tightly that some of it immediately ripped out. Joel gasped for breath and then, finally, retook control of his body. He looked up at Jeremy, who was stand-ing directly in front of the door, embraced by moonlight. Tears streamed down his face, and his eyes were bloodshot. Mats of hair were on the ground from where he had yanked them out, and blood was dripping from his head. He looked away from Joel, out into the moonlight.

Jeremy seemed calm for a moment, his hands dropping

to his side, a peaceful expression spreading across his face. "Don't you understand? They—they want me. They want the best for me. This is for the best." He slowly smiled, staring out the window.

Suddenly his eyes widened and he tensed, grabbing his head again, panic flooding his face. "No—NO! The sounds . . . I HAVE TO GET OUT! I can't escape—I have to listen—they COMPEL ME! I—"

BANG.

Joel was momentarily deafened by the explosion of sound, and the flash of light illuminated the entire room for an instant. Jeremy staggered forward, clutching his right shoulder. Joel looked down the hall, barely able to process what was happening. Emily stood at the other end, the gun from Joel's bag in hand. She began marching toward Jeremy, the gun still pointed at him.

Jeremy turned around and, after looking at Emily for a heartbeat, launched himself toward the door and flung it all the way open. Emily shot again as he lunged forward, but missed—Jeremy lurched out the door, falling to the ground. Emily quickly crossed the rest of the room and, reaching her arm out, helped Joel regain his feet. Joel covered his ears with his hands, grimacing in pain—the sirens were deafening with no barriers between them and him.

The two of them turned to look out the door—despite the only light outside being the moonlight, the outdoors seemed blinding and oppressive, as if the light was physically pushing back on anything it touched. Jeremy was crawling on the ground, leaving a trail of blood behind him from the bullet wound. Joel could see his chest heaving and, after a moment, realized that Jeremy was laughing.

After crawling about ten feet out from the door, Jeremy flipped himself over, facing directly up. He grabbed his head again with both hands, now covered with blood. Tears streamed down his face, and despite the fact that he was laughing uncontrollably, his eyes were stuck wide open, staring into the sky, and his arms and legs were twitching as if in horrible pain.

Jeremy's movements slowed, his laughter dying, as he stared up into the sky. Despite his injuries and being in such a frenzied state just moments before, he looked as though he was in utter peace. A smile slowly spread across his face as he started saying words, unheard to Joel and Emily.

Emily, reaching her arm across, slammed the door shut and locked it before grabbing Joel by his shoulders and bringing him back into the darkness, away from the window. She stashed the gun in her waistband before grabbing her flashlight and looking around frantically. She then darted back in front of the window and grabbed something off the floor.

She placed the flashlight on a shelf facing the two of them, then pressed his earplugs back in place. Joel exhaled in blissful relief as he was once again brought into comparative silence. Emily, shaking slightly, attempted to yell something at him over the noise, the words themselves lost but still mostly understandable by her mouth's movements.

"Are you OK? Did he get you with the box cutter?"

"No, I'm fine, I don't even think he tried. Just a bit dazed from the . . ." He motioned all around him, referring to the sirens. She breathed a sigh of relief, then responded.

"OK . . . good. We're fine. Sit down and try to clear your head; I'm going to make sure the door is shut."

Joel nodded and, very slowly, sat down with his back against a wall. Emily did as she said, firmly yanking the door a few times, then she pushed several boxes in front of it before returning to Joel. She sat on the opposite wall, then leaned her head back as well.

The sirens were still deafening to Joel, despite now having his earplugs in. The sounds pressed in from all sides, eventually forcing him into unconsciousness.

CHAPTER THREE

My mind felt numb. The weight…
The oppressive, all-consuming weight.
Any thought I had was held hostage by that terrible weight.
The weight of the unforgivable.

"Joel, hey—wake up! Are you still with me? We've got to get going."

As Joel came to, he felt a few firm nudges on his shoulder. He had a splitting headache, causing him to grimace and rub his head. Opening his eyes, he saw Emily standing in front of him, a concerned look on her face. "Yeah . . . yeah, I'm fine. What time is it?"

"Early—the sun just came up." She pointed toward the window, which was now luminescent with golden morning light. Emily reached her hand out to help him up. Joel winced at the jolt, his stiff muscles rebelling at the sudden movement, but he thanked Emily for the assistance. He looked around the room, the features of it much more visible in the overhead lights and the morning sun. As he suspected, the markings carved into the boxes extended all the way down the room.

He rubbed his head, his stomach in uncomfortable knots, as the events from last night came rushing back. Joel walked over to where their bags lay on the ground from the night before. He picked them both up and, handing Emily her bag, said, "Thank you, for last night. I would've been dead or worse without you."

Emily took the bag and then, holstering it over her shoulder, looked at Joel for a moment before responding, "Yeah, well . . . we've got to have each other's back during this. Now you owe me one, anyway."

Joel studied her expression as she said this—she was pale and looked nauseated. Guessing why, he cautiously asked, "Are you . . . OK? After what happened."

Emily began to say something, then stopped herself and just curtly nodded. She responded, not answering his question, "I'm more worried about you. I didn't see what happened, and you were pretty dazed last night. Are *you* OK?"

"Yeah, I'm fine. He had a grip on my neck for a few

seconds, but let me go before he did any damage. I don't think he wanted to hurt us, he just wanted to . . . get outside?" He raised an eyebrow as he waited for Emily's take.

"I'm not sure. It definitely looked that way, but . . ."

She turned and began walking toward the far end of the room, to the door that led outside. Joel, not following her immediately, called out, "Shouldn't we go back out the front? There might be . . . you know." Joel said the last part hesitantly, not wanting to finish the thought out loud. *There might still be a body right outside the door.* Emily stopped in front of the door, her hand on the knob.

"I know. Even if he is still there, I can't hide from it. But I don't think—" She flung open the door before she finished the sentence and, upon looking outside, exhaled heavily and closed her eyes. Joel quickly crossed the rest of the room and, standing beside her, looked outside as well. His eyes widened in shock: The pavement outside was completely clear.

Not only was Jeremy's body missing, even the blood on the ground had disappeared. It was as if the events of last night had never happened. Emily continued her broken sentence. "Just like the first night with the person I saw outside. He's gone."

What the hell is going on out here at night? The sirens are bizarre enough, but . . . how is that even possible? Emily and

Joel looked at each other, dumbfounded. After a few moments of silence, Emily shook her head and stepped outside, gesturing for Joel to do the same. He followed and looked toward the city. The outskirts of it were very close, just an hour or so away by foot, and from there he could find the theater where his mom and Ava were sheltered.

As he looked up at the high-rises of the downtown area, he felt anxiety bubbling up inside him. Not only would he finally be able to look for Ava and his mom, but they were approaching the epicenter of the disaster. *If Emily is to be believed about it starting in the middle of the city, anyway.* Joel and Emily quickly retraced their steps from the night before, returning to the highway before continuing their journey toward the city.

―――

As they reached the outskirts of the city center, with the first of the high-rises towering above them, Joel began to see several disturbing signs of life not present in the more sparsely populated suburbs. Aside from the roads now being in gridlock with stalled cars, all the buildings around them showed various signs of the chaos. Doors were broken off their hinges, cars were crashed into the sides of buildings. Despite all of this, however, there was not a single person in sight.

As Joel was observing these things, he felt Emily tap his shoulder and point up. "Joel, look. There's . . ." As her statement drifted off, Joel turned his gaze to where she was pointing. He felt the blood drain from his face as he looked up at the towering high-rises around them—most of the windows lining the upper floors were shattered. He quickly scanned the rest of the buildings in his line of sight, and they all showed the same thing. Joel and Emily looked at each other, disturbed. Emily quietly said, "What do you think that's about?"

"I don't know but . . . you saw what Jeremy was like last night. Do you think that . . . ?" Joel's question hung in the air as Emily glanced back up again at the shattered windows.

She shook her head after a moment. "No, that can't be right. It took Jeremy three nights to lose it. There's no way that there were people holed up in those buildings for three days without moving."

"Well, then what else could it be?"

They looked at each other in bewildered silence before Emily shook her head and, cautiously suggested, "Well . . . we could go inside one of them and see if we can find anything out."

Joel considered this for a moment, apprehensive. He wanted to search for Ava and his mom as quickly as possible, but they knew so little about the situation that it might be worth exploring.

Joel bit his lip and quietly said, "I don't want to waste time doing anything outside of finding my family."

Emily nodded empathetically, but countered, "I understand, but if they are safe and sound hiding away somewhere, I don't think an extra fifteen minutes will make a difference. What will make a difference is getting any information about what is actually going on here, so that all of us can be safer and know how to handle this."

Joel was silent for a moment, thinking, *She's right. And if I know my mom, she wouldn't take the initiative to get the hell out of there and try to run if she was panicked and worried. If she found a safe place to hide, she will be there until she knows it's safe to leave . . . or until someone finds her.*

Joel nodded, curtly saying, "Fine, but we need to make this quick. We can't search every room for survivors, just try to find anything obvious."

Emily nodded and, taking his response to heart, briskly turned around, beelining toward the closest building. Joel quickly followed, observing the features of it as he hurried after Emily. It looked like it was a fancy hotel, with somewhere around fifteen floors. When Emily reached the front door, she gave the handle a quick tug, and as the door effortlessly swung open, she turned around and quietly remarked, "Door's unlocked." She then crept into the lobby, looking around cautiously.

Joel followed her, also giving the room a cursory scan. It was a modern, sleek-looking lobby, with a set of elevators in the back, a fire-escape staircase to their left, and the reception desk to their right. All was silent around them, the building seemingly abandoned. Emily, looking back at him, said, "All right, let's see if we can find anything useful. Follow me."

Joel followed her as they walked back toward the elevators. He raised an eyebrow, saying, "Surely they aren't going to be working. This place is trashed, the electricity is probably cut off—" He stopped as Emily pushed the call button and a pleasant ding came in response as the doors opened. Emily smirked and, walking into the elevator, beckoned him in. They rode the elevator up several floors before exiting into a dark, gloomy hallway.

There was some sunlight streaming in through windows on either side of the building, but aside from those, the hallway was entirely unlit. The rooms lining the hotel hallway were in various conditions—some of the doors were still closed, some hanging open, and some looked as if they had been knocked off their hinges. And yet, despite the chaos, the hallways were eerily silent. After a moment of taking in the environment, Emily looked at Joel and said, "All right, let's split up and try to find anything useful. Look for people hiding out in rooms, look for notes, cameras left recording, anything at all that could help us figure out what's going on."

Joel nodded, then Emily turned around and cautiously walked down the hallway to the right. Joel turned to the left, and made his way to the first room. The door was still closed, and as he tried to open it, he found that it was locked. He put his ear to the door, listening. There were no sounds from inside the room. Frowning, he moved on to the next room, which had an open door. The furniture inside the room was strewn about. Chairs were knocked over, the bedding tossed around haphazardly, though the window was still intact.

After scanning the room briefly and finding nothing pertinent, he moved on to the next room. He wasn't even entirely sure what he should be looking for, but anything would be useful. The next room's door was also closed, but unlocked. He cautiously made his way into the room and, entering it, saw this one was in a significantly different condition than the last. The room was mostly undisturbed except the window was completely shattered. He approached the window and, looking closely at it, took note of several grisly details.

The window was broken mostly on the inside, with the outer parts fairly intact, albeit fractured and sharp. Bits of fabric were attached to some of the shards and, contrary to his initial suspicion, there was no blood on the jagged edges. He peered out the window, looking down at the pavement several floors below him.

As he was pondering the situation, he heard a yell from across the building: "Joel, come here! Quick! I found somebody!"

He spun around and, running as quickly as he could, made his way back down the hall. Emily was standing in front of a door, her ear pressed against it, jiggling the doorknob. As Joel approached, Emily turned a fraction toward him and, while continuing to tug at the door, said, "I can hear someone crying in the room. They won't respond, though."

Joel put his ear to the door, and, after a moment, heard the faint crying that Emily described. Unsure of what to do, he hesitantly called out, "If you can hear me, come open the door. We can help you. We just need you to open—"

Emily interrupted him, firmly saying, "Get out of the way." Joel turned and jumped as Emily aggressively kicked the door just below the handle. It didn't budge, but he heard a cracking sound. Emily stepped back and, giving a strained yell, kicked the door again, causing it to burst open. Emily disappeared into the room, and Joel quickly followed.

As he entered and looked around, he smelled something foul. The room was in chaos, with gouges in the wallpaper across the entirety of the room. A large man was sitting by the window, sobbing, gripping a large knife in one of his hands that dangled by his side. He didn't seem to notice their entry, his gaze fixed on the window. The window seemed to have fractures, but it remained intact.

Emily and Joel stopped, unsure of what to do. Joel called out again to the man, quietly asking, "Are you OK? What happened here?"

The man slowly turned his head before settling on Joel. His mouth trembled. Joel grimaced in sick realization as he saw the man's face, then the window behind it. His forehead was bleeding, shards of glass still stuck in his skin. The man then quietly said, "Please . . . Go. I need to stay here. I need to wait. They will be back soon."

Emily slowly asked, "Who will be back soon?"

The man smiled softly, as though lost in thought, before calmly responding, "My kids . . . I have to wait for them . . . They said they would come back."

Joel and Emily glanced at each other in confusion, before Joel took a step forward and said, "Just come with us for now. I'm sure they wouldn't want you wasting away here—"

Tears slowly streamed down the man's face as he shook his head. "No, no . . . I need to wait. They said they would be back. They said it would all be OK. This is for the best."

Joel raised his hands, inching nearer. "I really don't think they intended for you to . . ."

As he said this and moved closer, the man pointed his knife toward Joel, slowly saying, "You don't understand. I *will* wait for them."

Emily grabbed Joel's shoulder and gently, but firmly, pulled him away from the man. Emily backed up a few steps, still pulling Joel along with her, as she responded, "OK, we'll leave you alone. I hope they come back soon."

The man nodded, continuing to smile as he lowered his knife, and returned his gaze to the outside. He began slowly beating his head against the window, the glass crunching each time, blood dripping into a pool beneath him. Emily turned away, sickened, and quickly left the room. Joel recoiled, staring for a moment at the gruesome sight, before following Emily.

Emily reached in and, grabbing the knob, pulled the door shut, though it hung loosely from the hinges, the lock broken and the frame cracked. As they began walking back down the hall toward the elevator, Emily quietly muttered, "This was a mistake. Let's get the hell out of here."

Joel nodded as they entered the elevator once more. A few moments later, they were in the lobby again and soon made their way back out into the comfort of the afternoon sun.

Once outside, Emily quickly walked away from the hotel, down the road a few blocks. Eventually she stopped and they stood in silence for a minute, their minds reeling from the experience. Joel felt nauseous, everything else fading out as the adrenaline dissipated and he came to terms with what had just happened. He felt a nudge on his shoulder after a few moments, jolting him out of his thoughts. He realized Emily was staring at him, concerned.

"You still with me? You aren't responding to anything I'm saying."

Joel slowly nodded. "Yeah, sorry. That was just . . . a lot."

Emily's composure dropped for a moment as he imagined she was recounting the sight too, before she regained control and said, "Yeah, I'm sorry—we should never have gone in there. I just wish we could have helped him."

Joel, fighting away the nausea, quietly replied, "He was clearly deranged. We couldn't do anything to help."

Emily, looking particularly moved, asked, "I wonder why he thought his kids were coming for him? He looked like he had been there for two days straight, ever since this started."

"Maybe he thought that they had made it through the first two nights and were out looking for him. It's not impossible to assume, especially if they knew where he was staying before this all started. That's pretty much exactly what I'm doing."

Joel stopped for a moment, sickened, as a thought went through his head. *I just hope Mom is doing better mentally than the guy back there . . .*

Emily shook her head, lost in thought, before abruptly changing the subject and asking, "Well, now we are in the city center. What's your plan?"

Joel frowned, pushing her question aside in his mind for a moment. *How can she just move on from that like it was nothing? I . . . That was somehow even more disturbing than what happened with Jeremy. Jeremy was just completely insane, but this guy looked calm . . . happy.* Joel rubbed his forehead, trying to clear his mind, then replied, "Well, first and foremost, we need to get moving. We've wasted enough time here as is."

Joel let out a shaky breath and began walking again, trying to dispel the nerves. Emily quickly caught up to him and Joel continued, "I am going to find where my mom and my sister are. Based on the voicemails, they sheltered for the night at a movie theater. I know where it is; we used to go there all the time."

Emily nodded, a concerned expression on her face, then responded, "Well, I have nowhere else to go, so I'll come with you for now."

Joel nodded, relieved. "All right, well, then follow me. I know the way. It's not far from here." He began walking again, internally steeling himself for what he might find. Emily followed close behind, just as anxious for Joel's sake.

As they walked, Emily asked, "Who all are you looking for?"

"Just my mom and little sister."

Emily bit her lip, pausing for a moment, before asking, "How old is she? Your sister."

"She just turned six a few months ago. I . . ." Joel started to say something else, but cut off as he felt a lump form in his throat.

"I hope they are all right. I didn't have anyone else in the city when this all started, so I can't imagine what this is feels like."

"My mom will have kept her safe. She wouldn't have gone outside with her. I know she wouldn't have."

Emily nodded optimistically, and though Joel knew she was just being supportive, he appreciated it nonetheless. Glancing at her, he continued, "What's your plan, then? After I find my family."

"I'm not sure. I can't leave the city since the roads are blocked, so I guess I'll try to find any other survivors. I think I would be more likely to survive with a group all working together."

"If you want to, you know that you would be more than

welcome to come with us. You saved my life twice now; I owe that much to you. And aside from that, I think we make a good team. We started this whole apocalypse together; I think it's only fitting we make sure we both make it through the other side too."

Emily opened her mouth to say something but stopped, appearing to be touched by his words. She then simply smiled and nodded.

"I think that sounds like a good plan."

The next half hour passed in a haze. As Joel got closer to the theater, he could focus on nothing but his worries. Dozens of buildings passed without Joel noticing. *What if they aren't there anymore? Or what if they are, and are . . .* Joel sharply cut off the thought, shaking his head. Thoughts like that weren't going to help.

He looked up at all the buildings around him, the towering high-rises and skyscrapers blocking most of the skyline. He recognized where he was. The last time he had been here, just a week before, the streets were buzzing with life, the sheer amount of activity feeling claustrophobic and oppressive to him. But now, as he looked up at the lifeless buildings with shattered windows, and the streets filled only with stalled vehicles and wrecks, he felt a sense of loss for the place he once despised.

A few more miles passed in the blink of an eye, and suddenly Joel stood on the concrete pavement of the road, just a few dozen feet from the line of doors of the now abandoned theater. Most of the glass doors were shattered and hanging open. Emily was looking at him, concerned. Her voice cut through his mind. "Joel, you OK? You've been standing there for a minute." Joel tried to say something, but the words caught in his throat. He tried again, and, pointing, choked out, "This is the place."

Emily's gaze darted toward the shattered doors and the blood drained from her face. She stuttered for a moment before saying, "Come on, we need to go inside to check. I'm sure they are hiding out somewhere—this place is gigantic."

Joel, a burst of adrenaline flowing through him, leapt through one of the shattered doors and called out into the empty lobby, "Mom? Ava? Can you hear me?"

He could hear Emily faintly saying, "Joel! Be quiet, we don't know who else is here . . ." but the words passed through him without registering. He frantically looked around the lobby, seeing no signs of life. The floor was covered in scattered trash, and the furniture throughout the lobby was all tipped over or broken entirely.

Joel quickly ran through the lobby and began systematically searching through the different auditoriums, calling out into each one. Not only was he not getting a response from his mom or Ava, but the theater appeared to be entirely vacant of any life. Emily trailed behind him, searching as well, but her expression grew less and less hopeful as they went on.

Finally, after a good while of searching, Joel found himself back in the lobby, having checked every single corner of the building. He felt tears welling in his eyes as he stuttered, "We need to check them again, maybe we missed them somehow—"

Emily cut him off as she put her hand gently on his shoulder. "Joel, I don't think they're . . ."

Joel shrugged her hand off his shoulder as he stumbled forward, catching himself on the concession counter. His hands were trembling, a surge of emotion overpowering him.

They're not here.

CHAPTER FOUR

I looked over the edge, into that calling abyss.
The price that must be paid.
The burden I couldn't bear.
The sweet embrace of death.

Joel didn't even know what to think. He was scared to have hope, and yet too overwhelmed by grief at the thought that they might be gone to consider otherwise. Emily appeared next to him again and quietly said, "I'm sorry."

They stood there for a few moments before Emily continued, "They might still be out there, and the best way to find out is to find more people. If there is a group of survivors somewhere, that is the most likely place for them to be. Don't give up yet." Joel nodded, exhaling heavily. Emily pursed her lips for a moment before saying, "You can take a minute to collect yourself, but we need to keep moving and you need to keep your mind off the things we can't have any idea of knowing. I'll be waiting for you outside."

Emily stood for a moment before stepping back from him and walking across the lobby to cautiously exit through one of the shattered glass doors, out into the sunlight.

Joel nodded again, gathering his thoughts. *Maybe Emily is right. If they stayed put for the first night, then maybe they were able to find other people, or a place to stay safe.* The more he thought about it, the more certain he was that his mom would never have gone outside during the chaos, especially not with Ava. As these thoughts were running through his mind, Emily's voice split through the air. "Joel, come here! Quick."

Joel's head snapped up to see Emily leaning halfway through a door, frantically beckoning him forward. Joel ran across the lobby, and as Emily pulled him through the door, she pointed across the large parking lot toward the road on the other side.

Three people walking in the middle of the road, facing away from them. Each of them was carrying a large bag over their shoulder. Without a word, Emily began sprinting across the parking lot toward the group. Joel reached out for her shoulder as she ran past, but missed. He started after her, calling out, "Hey, wait! We don't know who they are, they might be—"

"Hey, HEY! Wait!" Emily's yell cut off his statement. The three stopped and turned around, startled, and set their bags on the ground. Joel swore to himself and trotted forward, attempting to catch up with Emily, who had sprinted ahead and now stood close to the group. As he approached, he heard Emily saying, "Who are you? Are you with a group? Are there other survivors? Are—"

One of the members of the group help up a hand, stopping her flow of questions. "Relax. Name's Jay. How long have you two been out here? Have you been . . . ?" He gestured toward his ears, raising an eyebrow.

Emily and Joel glanced at each other before Joel responded, "A couple of nights now, but yeah, we have had something to protect our ears. We were out here looking for family. Do you know if anyone from around this area is still . . . around?"

Jay glanced between the two of them, looking them both up and down, as though scanning for something. Jay then nodded and replied, "I don't know anyone specifically, but we are from a group of survivors. We are just heading back from a supply run—" He gestured toward the bags each of them had been carrying. "So, if you wanted to come with us, we could lead you back to them. Maybe you will find who you are looking for."

Joel immediately replied, "Yeah, absolutely, lead the way." Emily nodded in agreement, looking eager. Jay then picked up his bag and, gesturing for the others to do the same, said, "All right, then, follow me. It's a good walk from here, so settle in." They turned and began walking again, Joel and Emily following shortly behind. The group walked in silence for a few minutes before Emily spoke up, "So, what do you know about what's happening? We both know what to avoid, but we don't know . . . why."

Jay thought for a moment before responding. "We probably know about as much as you do. We know to protect our ears at night and to stay indoors, but not much else."

One of the other members, a burly-looking guy with curly hair, spoke up at that remark, quietly muttering, "The sirens at night aren't coming from us."

Jay snapped his head toward him, about to say something, before Emily interrupted, seemingly oblivious to the interaction.

"What do you mean they aren't coming from us? Someone has to set them off at night."

Jay continued staring at the other member of the group for a moment, who was now looking at the ground, before he cautiously replied, "We aren't supposed to tell people this immediately, so they don't panic, but . . . all the alarms and sirens going off at night aren't coming from any of us. No one is setting them off."

Joel and Emily looked at each other, unsure of what to say.

Jay, frowning, continued, "We don't know where they actually *are* coming from, though. Matthias is probably the guy who knows the most about what's happening. He has been gathering information on it from newcomers ever since it first started."

Emily, still stunned by the news, quietly asked, "Who's Matthias?"

"He runs the place. After the first night he was the one to rally the survivors and find a safe place for them to stay. There is an abandoned office building all of us able-bodied people are staying at, and over the past two days we have made it safer. Once we get back, I'll take you to him. He keeps a registry of everyone who is there, so that people who are looking for others can know whether or not they are with the group."

Emily looked back at Joel, who gave her a hopeful smile,

then resumed her questions. "How did he organize it so quickly? I could barely function the first night while it was happening, and the next day I was just scared and confused. It's amazing that he was able to help so many people so fast."

Jay's response was short and more irritated. "I don't know, I'm just here to do supply runs. You can ask him all the questions you want when we get there."

They fell into silence for a few moments before Emily dropped behind the others, matching Joel's pace. She quietly asked, "What do you think? About what he said about the sirens."

Joel, eyebrows furrowed in thought, replied, "It sounds crazy, but I had my own suspicions anyway. None of it makes sense to begin with, so I wouldn't write off the possibility."

"I had mine as well. Even though I had no other ideas, there was obviously something unnatural about it all from the very start."

Joel nodded, partially relieved that he hadn't been alone in considering that the sirens weren't normal. They fell into silence, and the group continued on, weaving through the grid of roads.

"All right, there it is."

The words snapped Joel back into reality. He had been lost in thought, mindlessly following the group. He looked up at the towering building before him, before quickly realizing it paled in comparison to the ones around it. It was much older than the more modern-looking skyscrapers—it looked to have only ten floors, and all the windows were covered from the inside.

As he stood there inspecting the building, the rest of the group had walked ahead to the door. Joel quickly caught up, and then entered. People were scattered around the foyer, some of whom waved wearily at the arriving group. Jay said something to the other two in the group, who nodded and walked off down one of the halls. He then turned to Emily and Joel, saying, "Welcome. Let me take you to Matthias to get your names down so you can ask any questions you have."

He turned and led them to an elevator, then pressed the button to call it. The elevator dinged pleasantly before opening. The three of them stepped in, and Jay firmly pushed the button for the tenth floor. The doors closed and, after a few moments, dinged again, opening to a new foyer, which had several people standing in various places.

All their gazes darted up to the three of them as the door opened. Jay nodded to them, and in return, they all turned their attention back to what they were doing. Jay then led them down a hall before stopping in front of one of the doors and knocking on it firmly. A few moments later, the door opened to a kind, if weathered, face.

"Ah, hello. Newcomers, I assume? Come on in, come on in. Thank you, Jay, you can go back to your room now." Joel and Emily turned and thanked him as well. Jay, giving a good-natured nod, exited the room and closed the door behind him.

Joel turned and observed the room. It was clearly a repurposed office, with a large desk in one corner, with three chairs situated in front of it. There was a makeshift bed in the other corner, and all the rest of the furniture in the room had been pushed to the side, apparently unneeded. The windows were plastered over with various objects, blocking most of the light, leaving the room illuminated only by the soft glow of a desk lamp.

Matthias made his way back to his desk, which was littered with papers and books. He sat down in the chair and gestured toward the chairs on the other side of the desk. "Please, take a seat, get comfortable."

Joel and Emily did as he requested, sitting in the two

front-most chairs. Joel observed the man in front of him—he looked middle-aged, which was strange because his hair and beard were almost completely gray and white. He was extremely pale with smile lines around his eyes, though he looked very tired. He reached into a drawer and pulled out a small notebook, then, grabbing a loose pen on his desk, looked up at Emily and Joel. "So, what are your names? I keep a list of everyone, just to help people find their friends and family." As they each said their names, Matthias quickly flipped between pages, writing them in place in what looked like an alphabetical list. As Matthias was doing this, Joel asked, "I actually am looking for family. Can you look for a 'Madison' and an 'Ava,' last name 'Walker'?"

Matthias looked up at him for a moment, a sad expression on his face. "Yes, of course, but, ah . . . not many people have made it to us. There are only a few hundred. So, keep your expectations . . ." He trailed off as he finished flipping through the book, stopping at *W*, then turning the book around toward Joel, pointed with his pen at a name. "Are these the ones you are looking for?"

Joel looked down at the list, and saw two names, written one after another. *Madison Walker, Ava Walker, Location #2.* Joel leaned back and put his hand over his mouth, tears welling up in his eyes as he slowly nodded in confirmation. He glanced at Emily, who looked equally relieved. She reached out and squeezed his shoulder in support. He looked back at Matthias, who was smiling kindly as he turned the book back toward him before addressing Emily: "Are you looking for anyone in particular?"

Joel looked at Emily, who simply shook her head in response, mouth firmly shut. Matthias nodded, looking back down at the book and tapping his pen on the two names. "Ah, I must let you know, Madison and Ava are at our second location. There is a safe house of sorts well outside the city center, a few hours' walking distance from here. It used to be some tourist attraction for a cave complex. Works quite well for our purposes, as all of those who are unable to gather supplies can rest safely down there without having to worry about the noise. The only issue is getting people from here to there, but I assure you they made it quite safely."

Joel opened his mouth, but Matthias continued, having anticipated his next question. "You won't be able to see them quite yet. We have no means of transportation over there other than on foot, so we don't risk anyone on the road unnecessarily. I will let you know the next time we are making a supply run, and you can see them then."

Joel scowled, raising an eyebrow in indignation at Matthias. "You don't want me to be able to see my family?

What's to stop me from just walking over there myself, alone, and taking the risk for myself? The only reason I'm here is to find them anyway."

Matthias gently shut the notebook and, putting it back in his desk, cleared his throat and calmly responded, "Well, I'm not going to tell you where it is precisely for that reason. If I told everyone where it was, this place would be vacant within the day and then there would be no one to help us gather supplies. I want all able-bodied people to stay and help gather food and other necessities for those who are unable to do so themselves—the only way we can survive long-term in these conditions is if we have a well-functioning community with rules and procedures. Seeing as you are both fit and healthy, I would appreciate you two choosing to stay here to help with gathering supplies for a while. I can't force you to stay, but you would be helping a good many people if you did."

Joel met Matthias's gaze coldly, not responding for a moment, before scoffing and saying, "OK, fine. Do you have a working phone, any way that I can at least talk to them to let them know that I'm here and OK? I would, but mine isn't working, neither is Emily's. Surely you have something? You can't just tell me that they're fine but then not let them know that I'm safe too."

Matthias shook his head and sighed, saying, "I'm afraid

not. It's not just both of your phones, it's, well, everyone's. The only way of getting a message from here to there is walking. But, if it puts your mind at ease, I will make sure that they are informed of your safety when we next send word to them. We need you here, though, at least for now."

Joel leaned back and sighed, rubbing his face with both hands. *He's right. With things being as dire as they are, I feel obligated to try to help. If I were there at the second location, I would be putting my hope in people doing the same for me. As long as I know Ava and my mom are safe, I'm content for now.*

Joel and Emily glanced at each other and, after a moment, they both nodded. Emily then replied, "We'll stay. We have a better chance here than we do on our own anyway."

Matthias smiled. "Good, very good. I must let you know, I have a few rules in place to keep things running smoothly. Since the power turns off at night, we have a tentative curfew in place to prevent people from getting stuck outside their rooms, since the elevators won't work. Aside from that, I'll send people to get you if you are needed for anything during the day. Speaking of . . ."

He shuffled through the papers on his desk for a minute before grabbing one and marking something on it with his pen. "Your rooms are 310 and 311. They won't have much in them right now, but you can ask anyone where the stockroom is. We have plenty of gathered bedding. That's all you need to know for now. Feel free to take the rest of the day off to get yourselves situated." Matthias smiled again and gestured toward the door.

Joel stood up, thanking him, but Emily remained seated and asked, "Wait, can you tell us anything about what all this is about? Jay said you've been doing research into it. We are working on theories right now."

Matthias regarded her for a second, before slowly responding, "I have done research, but I'm afraid it's just theories for now. Once I have more concrete information, I will update you all. Now, if you will excuse me, I have matters to attend to." He gestured again toward the door. Emily remained seated for a moment, seemingly unhappy with the answer, before getting up and, thanking him, exiting the room. Joel followed shortly, shutting the door gently behind him.

Emily was waiting for him outside with a strange look on her face. Joel raised an eyebrow in question as they began walking back down the hall. Emily then quietly said, "I don't like him keeping stuff from us. You'd think that any information is valuable in times like these, wouldn't you?"

"Maybe he just doesn't have anything useful yet. It's only been a few days, and he is probably even more stressed than the rest of us, trying to organize this community." They reached the elevator again. Emily pressed the button and, while they waited, replied, "I guess. Well, no matter what, I'm glad we at least have a safe place to stay for tonight."

The elevator dinged and the doors opened. Inside were two people—someone unknown, and Jay. Jay glanced between the two of them outside the elevator and tilted his head up in greeting as he escorted the presumably new person down the hall to Matthias's office. Joel and Emily then entered the elevator and Emily, as she pushed the button for floor three, said, "How are you feeling about the news about your family?"

Joel thought for a moment before responding. "Relieved, but I won't be without worries until I see them myself."

The elevator came to a halt and the doors opened, revealing yet another lobby with several people milling about. As they stepped out of the elevator, one of them approached the pair and asked, "Newcomers? What rooms are you in?" After each of them replied their respective number, he pointed down the hall to their left. "They will be down there, should be unlocked already. All the supplies are on the second floor, so go there after you get into your rooms to get whatever you need."

They thanked him, then walked down to their rooms. As they approached the two rooms, which were directly opposite each other in the hall, Emily stopped and turned to Joel, saying, "I'm glad we both made it here safe. Just knock if you need me for anything. Let's reconvene tomorrow morning and go from there, all right?"

"Sounds good. I'm glad we both made it here safe too. Enjoy the rest, I think we've earned it by now."

Emily smiled, then, opening the door, disappeared into her room. Joel turned to his door and did the same, and as he closed the door behind him, took a look at his temporary residence. Much like Matthias's, this room was very clearly an office—though this one hadn't been repurposed yet, with the exception of the large window by the desk that was painted over and covered.

As he thought about the idea of resting, he realized just how tired he was. For the past two nights, he had hardly gotten any sleep, and what he did get was marred and disrupted by the sirens. He stood there for a moment before promptly turning around and heading back out into the hall.

He walked to the elevator and took it down to the second floor. This time when the door opened, the lobby was empty. He stepped out and looked around—there were three hallways, one in front of him, and the other two at either side. On the wall next to each doorway leading to a hall were makeshift signs. The one to the left read FOOD AND WATER; the one in front of him, BEDDING, MISC. SUPPLIES; and the one to his right, SUPPLIES FOR SECOND LOCATION, the door for which was closed.

He walked into the hallway directly in front of him and, after having peered through several rooms, found a room with a variety of blankets and pillows. He grabbed a few of each, eagerly awaiting being able to sleep properly, then walked back to the elevator. As he waited for the elevator, he stopped and looked toward the storage hallway. Out of curiosity, he walked to it and attempted to open the door, but it was locked. Frowning, he turned back around and entered the elevator.

Once he returned to his room, he wearily moved some things around to make space in the corner for a makeshift bed, throwing a blanket on the ground to soften the carpeted floor. Despite the fact that sundown was still hours away, he slowly lay down and, without the stress of worrying about his mom and Ava, drifted off into the first peaceful sleep he had since this all started.

———

Joel jerked awake, his ears screaming, his head resonating as the deafening cries of the sirens began. His hands snapped up to his ears, trying to cover them, as he quickly realized that he had forgotten to put in his earplugs before he went to sleep. *Stupid, careless...* Berating himself, he fumbled around in his pockets until he found the plugs from the night before. He pushed them into place, exhaling in relief when the assault on his ears was mostly halted, though there was still an ever-present buzz and high-pitched whine in his head.

He looked around the room, adrenaline still coursing through him. It was mostly dark, but the window still glowed softly from the moonlight despite the coverings. He stood up, ears still ringing from the brief exposure. After a few minutes he sat back down and, putting his head against the wall, tried to relax again. Several minutes passed before something different cut through his mind, audible through all the other sounds.

"The following message is broadcast at the request of the United States government. This is not a test."

Joel slowly stood up again, looking around in confusion. *Where is that coming from? The power is obviously out, so it only could be coming from one place, but...* Joel walked toward the window, putting his ear on it, and continued listening.

"We warn all residents in this district to evacuate the city until further notice. Due to the uncertain facts of this civil emergency, we advise all residents to evacuate immediately. Protective action should be taken immediately. This is not a test."

The sound was coming from directly outside. Joel stepped back, dumbfounded, then quickly made his way to the door and, stepping into the hall, began knocking on Emily's door. The monotone emergency alert continued resonating in his head, though it was now quieter, as he was farther from any windows.

"Please stand by for this message from the Department of Homeland Security. Evacuate immediately. Evacuate immediately."

Joel swore to himself, realizing there was no way Emily would be able to hear the comparatively silent knocking, and opened the door himself. As he looked in, Emily was already awake, standing by the window. She spun around as Joel entered her peripheral vision, then her hands flew up and she mouthed, "What are you doing?"

Joel closed the door, and then, walking toward her, responded, "Do you hear it?"

She looked confused, raising an eyebrow. "Obviously. I think it's louder now that we are in the middle of the city."

Joel shook his head, agitated. "No, no, do you hear the emergency alert? The evacuation message?"

Emily didn't respond for a second, several emotions crossing her face as she looked back and forth between Joel and the window, before responding, "What are you talking about? All I hear are the sirens."

CHAPTER FIVE

Something else called my name, however.
A voice. The voice. Her voice.
The voice that took my hand and pulled me back from the
dark pit of my mind.
I wiped my tears away, smearing blood on my cheeks.
I looked up toward her voice.

Joel stepped back in stunned silence, his mind reeling. Emily was staring at him, with a confused and very concerned look on her face. Joel closed his eyes and directed his hearing toward the sirens again, but after a few moments, he realized that he couldn't hear the alert anymore. All that he heard was the usual, faint stream of sound that made it past his earplugs.

Joel felt Emily's hands as she grabbed him by the shoulders and guided him into one of the office chairs she had pushed up against the wall. Emily then turned and, reaching into her backpack, appeared to be looking for something. He sat down, dazed. *I . . . I heard it. I know I did. I even heard it over the sirens. Am I going crazy?* As the last thought entered his mind, Emily turned back around with a water bottle in hand and, squeezing it tightly, sprayed water on Joel's face.

Joel jumped and gasped, causing some of the water to go down his throat. Emily calmly turned around and put the pack over her shoulders. He started coughing, trying to clear the water from his throat, and as he wiped his face off, he angrily sputtered, "What the hell did you do that for?"

"Snapping you out of it. Come here." She mouthed at him over the deafening noise before grabbing his arm again and, yanking him up, led him out of the room. They walked down several hallways in the building, turning at seemingly random intervals, before she suddenly stopped and, opening a door, led him into complete darkness.

The sounds of the sirens, amazingly, became almost inaudible as Emily shut the door behind them. She guided him to the middle of the room, and after a moment, he felt her hands reach up and slowly pop his earplugs out. He recoiled, about to shout in objection, before he realized that the noise was *still* muted. Wherever they were, apparently it was far enough into the building, with thick enough walls, to protect them so that the sounds wouldn't be hurtful.

Her voice cut through the darkness. "We are safe here. I found this place earlier—it's a recording room. This whole part of the building is empty. No one is supposed to go back here, I think, because most of the windows on this side are broken. But we can actually hear each other in here." He heard some shuffling sounds from Emily before a bright beam of light appeared as she turned on a flashlight. "See?"

She pointed the flashlight at the walls of the cramped room, which were completely layered with industrial soundproofing. The only other things in the room were a microphone hanging from the ceiling in front of a small stand, and then what Joel assumed to be the control room on the other side of a glass panel. Emily looked at him, concerned. "So, what happened? I don't think I understood earlier—it was hard to tell what you were saying."

After Joel recounted what he had experienced, Emily remained silent for a moment before replying, "I definitely didn't hear any sort of spoken warnings, but it was louder than it had been before. Do you think it might be . . . affecting us?"

Joel was about to respond optimistically, but he stopped himself as he considered what they had experienced so far.

When he had listened to the sirens, even with ear protection, he had felt as if the sound was literally grating on his mind— as if it was crawling its way into his head and preventing him from thinking straight. And then, Jeremy—after just two full nights of listening to them with no protection at all—had gone completely insane.

Emily exhaled heavily, anxiously rubbing her face with both hands, having read his prolonged silence as a confirmation. Joel, seeing her distress, quickly said, "I think it probably has an effect, but we have no idea how bad it is or what it actually means for us. I only heard the alert once, and we haven't been exposed to it much after the first night, because of our earplugs. I think we just need to be calm, and take it one day—"

Emily sharply cut him off. "How am I supposed to calm down? You heard a message in the middle of the night, above all the rest of the sound, essentially telling you to go outside. And I know I'm being affected, because it's getting louder every night!" She stopped, her eyes darting to his for a moment, before continuing in a more collected tone. "I am going to find out what's going on. Matthias knows something, and we need to find out what it is. If it's actually, legitimately, causing us to go crazy over time, we need to know."

"What do you mean you are going to 'find out'?" Joel

waved his hand before Emily could respond, saying, "Never mind, just . . . if you are going to pry for more information, tread carefully. This is still the safest place for us to be, so we don't want anyone getting upset with us."

She nodded, then said, "I'll find a way. Right now let's try to get as much rest as possible, and not back in our rooms where we can hear the sirens. You stay here since you might be . . . might have been more exposed to the sounds than I have." She then handed him the flashlight and briskly walked out of the room. Joel walked to one of the walls and, putting his back against it, slid down into a seated position. A few minutes later, the door creaked open and Emily popped back in, arms filled with several pillows and blankets.

She walked over to him and, handing him his, quietly said, "Make sure to put your earplugs back in, just to make sure all the sound is blocked out. I'll have a plan by tomorrow. We'll figure this out." She walked to an adjacent wall and, after setting her things into position, lay down to sleep.

Joel did the same, laying down a blanket on the cold floor, before resting his head on the pillow again and trying to clear his mind. He pushed his earplugs back into place and, for the first time in days, was in truly blissful silence. Despite this, it took him a long time to finally fall into a tenuous sleep.

When Joel woke up, the interior of the room was visible, with the fluorescent white light of the hallways streaming in through the window in the door. Looking around, he quickly saw that Emily was still asleep. After a moment of indecisiveness, Joel decided to let her continue sleeping and, walking toward the door, cautiously pulled his earplugs out, which was met with silence. He gently opened the door and, closing it behind him, began wandering down the hallways.

He had no memory of the path that Emily had taken to get them to that room last night, especially since it had been mostly in the dark. After several minutes of aimlessly strolling, he finally heard activity down one of the paths—the faint, layered murmur of several people speaking. Joel, making his way toward the noise, soon entered into the lobby next to the elevator, though from the other direction than his room was.

A small group of people were standing by the large window of the lobby, talking while basking in the sun. As Joel approached, one of them turned and politely nodded in greeting before turning back to the group. Joel returned the gesture, then after making his way to the elevator, waited patiently for it to arrive. His mind was troubled, the events of last night still bouncing around in his head.

"Joel? Is that you?"

Joel's head snapped around toward the voice and he was met with a familiar face, which lit up in recognition. Facing him was a girl about as tall as him, with warm sepia skin, thick curly black hair going all the way down her back almost to her hips, and a wide smile on her face.

Joel's eyes widened as his mind was thrown back several months to high school. He hadn't talked to her much at the time, but he definitely recognized the girl in front of him. "Kayla?"

Kayla darted forward and hugged him tightly, before stepping back and smiling sheepishly. "It feels so good to see a familiar face around here in all this chaos! No one else I know is here." Her face dropped for a moment as she said this, but she seemed to quickly dispel the negative thoughts.

Joel nodded, returning the smile. "Yeah, it's good to see you here too! I'm glad you made it through the last couple of nights safely. Have you been here since the start?"

The elevator dinged pleasantly as the door opened, allowing Joel and Kayla to step inside after a small group of people exited. Upon entering, Joel hit the button for the ground floor and Kayla cheerfully replied, "I haven't been here, like, in this building, since the start—I got here on the day after that first night. But I've been in the city for the whole time, yeah."

After a few moments the door opened again, and Joel stepped out, Kayla close behind him. The lobby was mostly empty right now, aside from a couple of very tired-looking men by the door. Joel quietly said, "Hold that thought for a second—let's see if these guys know what the procedure around here is."

As he and Kayla approached, one of the men held up a hand and, after blearily staring at Joel, slowly said, "We wouldn't advise you to go out without a group. If you come back in about an hour, groups will be organizing in this lobby. So just . . ." His statement drifted off as he yawned, lifting a hand to his mouth.

Kayla pursed her lips in sympathy, asking, "Night shift?"

The two men nodded, then one of them said, "If you thought the sirens were bad already, try having to sit out here and listen to them all night long without sleeping at all. Almost done, though. Our shift ends once everyone starts leaving this morning."

Kayla smiled at them, cheerfully replying, "Oh good! I hope you sleep well once it's over."

As they nodded in appreciation, Joel and Kayla turned around, walking back toward the elevator. As Joel was thinking about what to do to occupy his time, Kayla asked, "So, do you want to go get breakfast?"

Joel raised an eyebrow at the suggestion, asking, "Where do you suppose we do that?"

As they entered the elevator, Kayla reached past him and pushed the button for the second floor. "Trust me. We are about to experience the height of luxury."

A couple of minutes later, they were walking out of one of the supply rooms, two granola bars for each of them in hand. As they passed back through the lobby, Kayla happily began eating the first of hers.

They sat on the floor of the lobby, backs against one of the walls, as they ate their meager breakfast.

Joel, recalling where they had left off the conversation, said, "So, you've been in the city from the start? How did you end up here?"

Kayla frowned for a moment in thought and, after swallowing a bite of food, slowly said, "Well, it's been a tough time. Since I moved out and got my own place, I was alone when it all happened on the first night. The first thing I did the next day was leg my way over to my parents' place, but both of them were gone by the time I got there. I wandered around the city for a bit on foot after that, not really sure what to do with myself, and that's when a group of people found me and told me about this place and brought me here. What's your situation looking like?"

Joel exhaled slowly and, shrugging, quietly said, "Honestly, pretty much the same story as yours. My mom and sister came into the city to go see a movie, I stayed at home out in the country because I had a headache, and I came here the next morning once I heard what had happened. In my search we stumbled across people who brought us here. But I think it's going to be OK; Matthias says that he has them down on his list and that they are safe at the second location, out of the city. Do you know if . . . ?" Joel let his question hang, unable to finish the thought.

Kayla smiled at him, her mood seeming to brighten. "Yup! My folks are safe and sound there too. I'm not sure why Matthias didn't have them stay here to help gather supplies, but according to him I just barely missed them. The big expedition he made out to the second location with the first batch of arrivals apparently left only an hour before I got there." Her face dropped again as she added, "My brother wasn't on the list, though. I hope he's OK."

Joel nodded thoughtfully, asking, "How old is your brother? Was he with your parents?"

Kayla let out a small laugh, shaking her head. "No, no— he is older than me, he has a stable job and is engaged and everything. He's smart, I'm sure he found a good place to stay safe with supplies."

Joel nodded politely, hoping for her sake that her optimism would turn out to be true.

They sat in silence for a minute, Kayla eating and Joel staring at the floor in front of them, lost in thought from the conversation. Kayla, having finished her food, broke the silence by saying, "Hey, I have an idea. There was this cool place I found in this building yesterday, I think it might brighten the mood a bit."

She suddenly bounced up and reached her hand out to help him up. Joel, caught off guard, stared at her hand for a moment before taking it. Once he was up, Kayla let go and, after making her way to the elevator, pushed the call button. By the time Joel walked across the room after her, the door had opened. Once inside, she pressed the button for the top floor. Joel, confused, slowly said, "I don't know if we are supposed to be up there; that's Matthias's floor. They've got management stuff up there."

"I know, but there is something else up there too. I'll show you." A few moments later, they arrived at the top floor. As Joel suspected, the posse of guards from before were standing in the lobby, all of whom stood up and focused their attention on Joel and Kayla. One of them called out, "What are you doing up here? Unless you want to talk with Matthias about something important, this is off-limits."

Kayla, making a pouty face, replied, "Oh, well, we were just going to go upstairs to get some fresh air. Is that OK? I'm sure you wouldn't mind, right?" She smiled sweetly, looking hopeful. The man appeared conflicted for a moment before sighing and waving them on.

Kayla looked back at Joel and winked, then beckoned him forward. They began walking down the hall to the left, opposite the direction that led to Matthias's room. A minute or two and several hallways later, they approached a small staircase leading up to the roof of the building. Kayla opened the door and walked outside, the morning sun filling the staircase. Joel followed her, shutting the door behind them.

He closed his eyes for a moment as he breathed in the crisp air, and the autumn breeze washed over him. When he opened his eyes, Kayla was standing near the edge of the roof, smiling back at him. He joined her, and they looked out over the city together. The sky was glowing brilliantly as the sun bloomed on the horizon, orange and yellow slowly giving way to blue, painting the clouds above them a soft reddish-pink. The colors reflected off the buildings, magnifying the beauty all around them.

They stood there for a few minutes in silence, soaking it all in. Joel, for the first time in days, felt peaceful. As he stared out at the sunrise, all his worries and stress washed away in the breeze. Kayla eventually sat down on the edge of the building, her feet dangling over the side. Looking up at Joel, she patted next to her. Joel slowly lowered himself down and joined her.

After a moment, Kayla said, "Even though there's a lot going on, I think taking a minute to just enjoy the breeze and the view can help with the stress, right? It always makes me feel better."

Joel thought about her words as he looked out at the horizon. *It's amazing that she can still find things to be grateful about, even in the middle of all this madness. Even just these few minutes with that perspective have helped me a lot.* The two of them sat in silence, enjoying the brief reprieve from reality.

Sometime later, Joel stirred, saying, "We should probably get back down to the lobby now. Don't want to be late." He carefully scooted back from the ledge before standing, then offered his hand to Kayla, who gladly took it. As he helped her up, he added, "And thank you for bringing me up here."

Kayla smiled at him and nodded. They made their way back to the door, then through the quiet halls to the elevator. They rode it down to the main lobby again.

After glancing around the room—which was now mostly filled with people, all organized into small groups—he saw

Jay standing near the door with a group of five people around him. Joel weaved through the people in the lobby, and as Jay saw him approaching, he raised a hand in greeting. Joel then said, "Hey, you're just the guy I'm looking for. Who organizes all these groups to go out to get supplies and whatnot? I don't know what I'm . . ." Joel's statement drifted off as he saw Jay was looking at him, smirking.

"*I'm* the guy organizing the groups, so you came to the right place. You can come with me today, one of our people is MIA." Joel was about to respond, when he heard Kayla's voice from behind him.

"What about me? I don't have a group yet either, so can I come along?"

"Well . . . My group isn't going to be collecting supplies, we are doing something else. We have word from a trustworthy source that there is information about the sirens, in a corporate building for an off-site testing facility. Theory is that one of their experiments might have been the epicenter of this disaster. Since we will be scouring drawers and filing cabinets for papers anyway, by all means, the more the merrier."

Kayla gave an enthusiastic thumbs-up to Jay, before playfully nudging Joel's shoulder. "I wasn't going to let you get away from me that easy."

Joel gave her a small smile before returning his attention to Jay. After a few moments, Jay put his fingers to his mouth and whistled, causing the room to go silent. He then called, "All right, let's get a move on. Stay safe, don't be dumbasses, and be back before dark. We've got families to care for, so let's do it." He then turned and briskly led the way outside.

Joel and the rest of the group followed after Jay, and Joel heard behind him the sounds of everyone else shuffling toward the door. They broke out into the morning sun, and after making their way onto the road, Jay promptly led the group left. Looking behind them, Joel saw a continuous stream of people exiting the safe haven, all going in different directions out into the city, all with the same purpose.

Jay began calling out to the group as he walked. "All right, our destination is about two hours away. I don't know how big this place is, but that should be plenty of time to get what we need and get back. We have plenty of food and water with us, so this should be an easy day."

Kayla materialized by Joel's side again, cheerfully asking, "So, what do you think about all this?"

Joel glanced at her, startled for a moment by her sudden appearance, before replying, "What do you mean?"

"You know, all of it. The sirens at night, this little community, the fog, the animals—"

Joel looked at her, his attention now fully on what she was saying. He cut her off, asking, "Animals? What do you mean? I haven't seen a single animal since I got here."

Kayla's bubbly demeanor dropped as she replied, "Oh, you don't know? Well, now there aren't any animals, but on the first night there were. I watched them out my window. I felt bad for the poor things."

Joel didn't know how to respond for a moment, confused, before replying, "Well, what happened to them?"

"I don't know, I didn't watch for long. There were little birds on my porch, underneath the overhang so they could be in the shade during the day. It was really weird . . . Even though I could barely stand how loud it all was, they didn't seem to notice it. But after a couple of minutes, they suddenly just . . . flew out into the street. Right after they did, though, they fell onto the street and just lay there, not moving."

Joel thought about her story, his eyebrows furrowed in confusion. Before he responded, Kayla continued, "I think it just got into their little heads really fast. I wonder what they heard—obviously we hear the sirens and sometimes the voices, but since they weren't scared maybe it isn't an actual noise . . ."

Whatever she said after that was lost as Joel's mind reeled from her casual mention of the alerts. He then cut off her statement, exclaiming, "Wait, you hear the emergency messages too? The voice saying something about a civil disaster and to evacuate?"

Kayla looked at him, confused. "Yeah, doesn't everyone? I didn't hear them on the first night, but I heard them a bit on the second night, and then last night even more. I only heard the stuff you are talking about on the second night, though. Last night it sounded more like a person, saying something about getting outside, the indoors weren't safe, something about it being for the best that I listen, all of that. The weird thing was the voice sounded familiar."

Her voice trailed off, appearing disturbed by her own recollection, then she shook her head and nonchalantly said, "I'm not too worried about it. If I go crazy, then at least I don't have to listen to those awful sounds anymore, right?"

Joel stammered, unsure how to respond. *If she is hearing them too . . . At least that means I'm not being affected by it in a way that other people aren't. But, actual voices? That's . . . concerning.* He responded, "I . . . Well, I think they affect whoever listens to them for too long, but you seem pretty clear of mind, so I wouldn't worry about losing it just yet."

They fell into a thoughtful silence as the group continued weaving their way through the lifeless city.

A couple hours later, Jay stopped and held up his hand,

prompting everyone else to stop as well. Reaching into his backpack, he pulled out what looked like a map and then looked up in bewilderment at a towering skyscraper, across an intersection from where they were.

Several steps led up to a series of six glass double doors, one after another, above which a logo that Joel didn't recognize was displayed. The entire wall of the first floor was glass, showing a sleek, modern lobby. Several of the doors were shattered, and there were fractures webbing out across several parts of the wall. After a moment of stunned silence, Jay called out, "Well . . . this is the place."

CHAPTER SIX

The moon was so beautiful that night.
I was so enraptured by it, nearly all other thoughts washed away.
Nearly.
I struggled to remember why I had looked.
I struggled to think of why I should look away.

Emily groaned as she opened her eyes, still exhausted. She had no idea how long she had stayed up last night, ideas and plans rolling around in her head. As she pushed herself from the ground, she looked around the room and, seeing Joel was already gone, frowned. While her plans didn't involve him actively, she still would have liked to at least say goodbye as he went out for the day. She shook her head, then made her way out of the room.

The hallways were silent, which was to be expected in this part of the building, but even as she drew closer to the populated areas, she didn't hear any activity. She stopped by her room to grab supplies, and as she approached it, she saw the door was still open from last night. The disturbing things Joel said he experienced came rushing back to her, troubling her. *I don't even know what this means for Joel, but I need to find out what Matthias is hiding.*

While she was in her room, she quickly gathered a few of her things—a small notebook, a pen, and a small, ornate knife—and put them into her pockets before heading back to the elevators. She looked down at her old-fashioned watch, which read a quarter past ten. *People should already be out for their supply runs by now. Now's the time.* She took the elevator down to the first floor, revealing a mostly empty lobby with two people by the front door. As she approached, they both held up a hand, one of them saying, "We don't recommend you go outside without—"

Emily waved her hand, interrupting him. "I'm not going anywhere; I just want to know where everyone is. I had a few questions for Jay, if you know where he is in particular."

They both looked at each other, not responding for a moment, before one hesitantly said, "Well, Jay is out right now, some sort of mission to a testing facility. Apparently, they think they can find information there. Everyone else is out on supply runs."

Emily internally scoffed. *Yeah, leading a group to find*

intel. Sounds about right. Emily half-heartedly thanked them, then turned back, frowning.

She took the elevator up to the second floor, ideas floating around her mind. She was startled as the elevator door opened, revealing a person waiting on the other side. They paid her no mind as they entered the elevator and went on their way, but their presence still made Emily paranoid.

She approached the door labeled SUPPLIES FOR SECOND LOCATION. The door was still closed and locked, as she suspected. After a cursory glance around the room, making sure there was no one else there, she took out her knife and attempted to pick the lock. She was out of practice, but given enough time she should be able to get it open. After a minute of her fidgeting with it, she heard a voice behind her yell, "Hey, what are you doing?" She spun around to see a man standing there, having emerged from the food and water supply room.

After a moment, she recognized him as the guy who had spoken up about the sirens after they found Jay. He approached her, saying, "You aren't supposed to go in there; don't you know what that's for? It's locked for a reason. There's plenty of food back there." He gestured with his thumb behind him.

Emily, squinting at him, put her knife back into her pocket and, avoiding the question, said, "I know you—why did you tell us about the sirens when Jay didn't want you to? He made it seem like it should have been pretty clear to you not to do that."

He looked uncomfortable, rubbing the back of his neck with one hand. "Well, uh, I just thought you should know. I don't agree with some of the things they are doing. But that doesn't—"

Emily cut him off, asking, "Oh? Is there anything else I should know about?"

His gaze returned for a heartbeat to the room behind her, before he sighed and beckoned her forward as he walked toward the elevator. She hesitated, then followed. As they entered the elevator, the man quietly said, "If anyone else caught you trying to get in there, you would have gotten kicked out. I'll try to help you, but you can't take risks like that. My name's Chris, by the way."

Emily raised an eyebrow as he pushed the button for the top floor. "Where are you taking me?"

"Somewhere we can talk in private."

Emily didn't push the subject, but remained tense. As the elevator doors opened, only one other person was in the lobby. They nodded a greeting to Chris, who returned the gesture before leading Emily to a room down the hallway to the left.

They entered a small room with nothing in it but a desk

and a makeshift bed, made of nothing more than a layer of cardboard to shield against the cold ground, a small blanket, and a pillow. Emily closed the door behind them but remained by it. Chris walked into the room and sat down on the makeshift bed before saying, "You'd better come in here—don't want anyone overhearing this."

After a moment, she cautiously walked farther into the room and stood, leaning against a wall, with one hand resting on the knife in her pocket. Chris then said, "I probably don't know much more than you do; Matthias keeps information very close to his chest and shares it with only a few of his trusted people. But, being directly under those people, I have learned some things."

Emily waited for him to say more, but he remained silent. She raised an eyebrow, prompting, "Well? What are those 'things'?"

Chris looked hesitant, but quietly said, "I don't know much, and what I do know isn't concrete. But, if you are looking for possible clues, the sirens aren't the only thing out there at night. I have only heard whispers behind closed doors about it, but there is a reason we can't go outside at night, even with earplugs and all the noise-canceling headphones we could wear."

Emily thought about it for a moment, before her eyes

widened in revelation. "Maybe that's why the sirens draw people out, getting into their heads to make them go outside. The sirens themselves aren't the danger, they draw people *into* the danger." *And, from what Joel told me last night, they are getting better at it too. First all they do is mimic sirens and emergency alarms to try to scare people and get them to flee in panic, but now they are changing. Joel heard an actual message telling him to go outside, even if it wasn't a real voice.*

Chris nodded slowly, deep in thought. He replied, "That makes sense, but I don't know what we can do about it. Our situation doesn't change."

Emily bit her lip, thinking. He was right—this didn't change anything if it was correct, other than confirming that Matthias was truly hiding important information. She changed the subject, asking, "What about Matthias? Do you know where he might keep his research notes, or . . . ?" Her question drifted off, as if she did not know for sure what else she might be looking for.

Chris hesitated, looking concerned, before replying, "Well, I don't know about any 'research notes,' but I will say that he doesn't sleep in that office of his."

Emily raised an eyebrow, wondering how that could possibly be relevant, before she remembered that Matthias had a bed in that office. "So then, what, the bed of his in there is just for show?"

"I think it's to not draw any suspicion, but I know for a fact that he isn't in that room at night. The first night I was here, I was restless for obvious reasons, so I was wandering down the halls trying to get my mind off everything, but I noticed that his door was open. I went and peered in, and he wasn't in there. I checked again the next night, but the door was closed and locked. I can't shake the feeling that it being open the first time was a mistake."

Emily rubbed her chin thoughtfully. *It could just be a coincidence—the first night he actually might have just been wandering around and then after that he was just in his room.* "Is there anything else you know?"

"Not really, no. To get any more, you would have to get it from Matthias himself or from his own notes."

"How do I get a meeting with Matthias?"

"He isn't just going to give you the information if you ask politely. I don't know what you expect to happen."

Emily scowled at him, and after a moment, Chris sighed and continued. "Just go knock on the door. He is always in there, doing something or another. Someone will probably stop you from just waltzing in, but just tell them that you have concerns you want to bring up with Matthias and I'm sure he will see you."

Emily nodded and turned to leave the room. As she exited, she looked back and said, "Thank you for your help. If I find anything, I'll let you know."

"No problem. Good luck."

Emily shut the door behind her and made her way back down the hallway toward the lobby. As she was halfway down the hallway, she saw the lone person from before still standing guard. She approached him, saying, "Hey, I need to speak to Matthias. It's urgent."

The guard, raising an eyebrow at her, asked, "Why?"

"I have information that might be useful to him. About everything that's going on."

He shrugged, then beckoned her to follow him. After a short walk down the hallway, he knocked on Matthias's door, calling out, "Hey, boss, a resident wants to speak to you. Something about intel."

A few moments later, the door creaked open, revealing Matthias's kind face. He looked preoccupied, but smiled, saying, "Ah, yes, Emily, I remember you from the other day with that Joel fellow. Come in, come in."

He opened the door fully, gesturing for her to sit down in

one of the chairs. As she entered, the guard closed the door behind her. Matthias slowly sat down in his chair on the other side of the desk before quietly saying, "So, Emily, you have some sort of information for me?"

She sat down, quickly scanning the room as she did so. The makeshift bed was still in one corner, looking pristine with the blanket tucked in over the pillow. The windows at the far end of the room were painted over and covered, just like all the others in the building. The unneeded furniture remained pushed against the walls. The only things of interest in the room were the bed and the desk.

Realizing she hadn't responded, she looked at Matthias, quickly replying, "Yeah, well—It's more of a concern, and I was hoping either you could shed some light on it, or that this might be new information entirely that is useful."

Matthias reached for a notebook as she said this and, opening to a blank page, clicked his pen in preparation to write. "By all means, continue."

"Well, Joel, that friend of mine from the other day—I'm worried about him. The other night he came into my room, started talking about hearing voices and whatnot. I don't know if the stress is getting to him, or if he is being affected, maybe? Do you have any idea?"

She asked this, already knowing full well that Joel was being affected by the sirens, but she just needed a topic to bide time while she looked for anything useful. She studied the desk—the papers and notebooks on it were still scattered about haphazardly, but the ones that faced her showed nothing interesting—lists of names, quantities of items they had in store, and schedules for supply runs. There were other papers that had much more tightly written, scrawling text, and what looked like drawings of some kind, but they were mostly covered by the other things on his desk.

Matthias, speaking as she observed these things, replied with a frown, "I'm sorry to hear he isn't doing well. It certainly isn't impossible that the sirens are affecting him; several other people have reported similar things." He tilted his head slightly as he watched her eyes dart around his desk. "Are you all right? You seem . . . preoccupied."

She looked back up at him, panic momentarily jolting through her, before quickly saying, "Yeah, sorry. My mind is just wandering all over the place. This is all a lot to take in already, but are you telling me that we might be, like, going crazy? Why didn't you tell us before?"

Matthias sighed, closing his notebook and setting his pen down. "There is a fine line between informing people and inciting panic. People are already dealing with enough stress and anxiety as it is. I don't need to layer on the possibility that we all might be being mentally affected by them too."

They stared at each other for a moment in silence before Emily responded, changing the subject, "Do you have any word from the second location? Joel is anxious to see his family."

The room itself was devoid of any clues, so now she searched him, looking for any sign of a crack. His gray hair and beard were well groomed, considering the circumstances, and though he looked tired, he was obviously in a normal state of mind. She saw his eyebrow twitch for a moment before he responded. "I assure you that they are all doing quite well. If you would like, next time I schedule a run down there, I can arrange for you to go as well. That being said, I'm not entirely sure if I would be comfortable sending Joel down, with what you are saying about his mental state taken into consideration."

She raised an eyebrow, sharply responding, "I would think that letting him see his family might help him."

Matthias regarded her for a moment, not responding, before sighing and standing up. "I'll see what I can do. For now, if you would excuse me—I need to discuss some things with my team in a few minutes."

He began walking toward the door, passing Emily. The moment he stepped by her, she stood and, as the chair squeaked against the linoleum floor, she snatched one of the papers she hadn't been able to decipher before. Creasing it, she put the paper in her waistband and covered it with her shirt. Matthias didn't seem to notice—as he reached the door, he opened it with a tired smile and simply gestured for her exit.

She walked through, attempting to look as casual as possible, giving a quiet thank-you as Matthias shut the door behind her. She sighed, closing her eyes for a moment, before walking back to the elevator. The office seemed normal, the items on his desk mostly seemed normal, and most importantly, he seemed normal—and, for those reasons, she was now entirely convinced that he was hiding something.

She entered the elevator and, after taking it down to the third floor, quickly made her way back to her room. Upon entering, she firmly shut the door behind her and, after locking it, quickly pulled the paper from her waistband and set it out on her desk. She sat down and began studying it.

The front of it was packed with dates, times, and activities, which she assumed was a schedule of supply runs. She frowned, hoping to have grabbed something revealing. She turned the paper over to find a drawing of sorts. After a moment, she realized it was a crudely sketched map.

Near the center of the map was a small circle, labeled *B*. North of it, across several rows of squares and lines that she assumed to be buildings and roads, crisscrossing in the grid of the city, was another circle, labeled *V.* Far to the east of the *B* was another circle, labeled *2.* Aside from those three, the map was unlabeled, simply showing a rough top-down view of the roads and buildings of the city around them.

She frowned, imagining that B was their current location, at home base, and that the 2 was the second location where the families stayed, but she couldn't think of anything that made sense for the V. Not only that, she hadn't even heard anyone mention a third building. *I'm going to find out what they are hiding there.* She folded the paper again and, after putting it into her pocket, made her way out of her room and back to the elevator.

As she exited on the ground floor and approached the front door, she held up a hand and stopped the two guards from talking. "Yeah, I know. Not supposed to go out without a group, it's dangerous, all of that. It's daytime, I'm an adult, I'm going out."

The two looked at each other, flabbergasted, before silently stepping aside. She walked past, through the doors, and out into the blinding sunlight.

She made her way a few streets north, well out of sight of the base, before she pulled out the map. It was hard to tell exactly how far away the V on the map was from her, but she was confident she could find it just by counting streets. As she walked down the lifeless streets, she enjoyed the chilly breeze and the contrasting warmth from the sun. Having been cooped up inside for more than a day, she was glad to finally be outside again.

About an hour later, Emily finally turned onto the street that she believed contained her destination. She had walked past it the first time and had to double back, but if the crude map was an accurate representation of the streets, this should be the one. She looked closely on at the map—the V was the eleventh building down the street from where she believed she was.

She began walking down the street, anxious about what she might find. She wanted to be right, to prove that Matthias had some part in all this and knew more than he let on. But at the same time, if that were true, then their situation would be much worse than they thought.

As these thoughts were rolling around her mind, a sudden eruption of sound down the block startled her. She instinctively jumped to the side, off the sidewalk, and into a small alleyway. The noise didn't dissipate, and sounded strangely familiar. She closed her eyes for a moment, listening closely. In fact, it seemed to be getting louder and closer. After a moment, she realized what it was—it was the sound of a *motorcycle*.

Her eyes widened, possibilities bouncing around her head, but she remained hidden. The sound of the engine was quickly approaching. A few moments later, the motorcycle soared past on the empty sidewalk. She couldn't make out any details of the rider before they drove out of sight.

She remained in the alley for a moment, gathering her thoughts. She pushed the questions about what she just saw aside for the moment, focused on getting to the building on the map. She slowly peeked her head out of the alley before resuming walking down the sidewalk. There was no more activity to be seen or heard—just the one random rider. She counted buildings as she went, and a minute later, she saw her destination. It was a parking garage.

She approached the front entrance of the parking garage, listening closely for any more signs of activity. She slowly walked in; there were vehicles of many varieties parked all across the garage from before the sirens started, but she didn't know how that would help her—or any of them, for that matter—since they didn't have the keys to any of them, and the roads themselves were blocked.

She started making rounds around the garage, going up floor by floor, looking for anything useful. It didn't make sense for this place to be specifically marked on the map if there was nothing here. As she approached the top level of the garage, she began losing hope. She finally reached the top, and as she gave a cursory scan of the floor, her eyes landed on something suspicious.

She weaved her way through the rows of cars and, after a moment, emerged in front of a small collection of sleek motorcycles, parked in the middle of the lane. There was a small bucket lying next to them, with a piece of paper attached to it. She approached it and, picking up the bucket, read the paper: "Return the vehicle here once you finish and put the key back in the bucket."

Peering into the bucket, she saw several keys lying in the bottom of it. Dumbfounded, she picked one of them up and clicked a button on it that displayed a set of lights. Immediately, the headlights on one of the motorcycles in front of her blinked rhythmically several times before turning off. She put the bucket down and backed up, mind reeling.

They have a ton of working motorcycles. How? Why? And . . .

Her train of thought paused and her eyes widened as her mind rested on a chilling question.

What is Matthias using them for that needs them to stay a secret?

CHAPTER SEVEN

But . . . that voice. She dragged me back to lucidity.

I tore my eyes away from the silver radiance in the sky.

I looked toward the voice, but my gaze passed over the remains.

The remains of what I had done.

The remains of what little joy and happiness I had in my life.

As they approached the building, Joel heard Kayla mutter, "We are going to be here all day." The doors were unlocked, so Jay simply picked one of the ones that hadn't been shattered and cautiously led the way in. Once inside, Joel looked around—the lobby was enormous, with several sets of elevators on either side, and a large staircase in the back leading up to the individual floors.

It might have been awe-inspiring had it not been marred by the effects of the disaster. Aside from the shattered windows, the furniture in the lobby was strewn about chaotically, and several of the elevators had been jammed open with various items. Documents lay scattered around on the ground, some with grimy shoeprints facing toward the doors.

Jay called out, "We are looking for any intel about the sirens. Spread out, scour every room of this place. We have a lot of space to get through and not much time." Jay paused for a moment, then added, "And if you find any survivors hiding out, let me know immediately. They will probably be scared and starving, so we need to get them out of here."

All the members of the group responded, but after a moment, one of them yelled, "Hey, these elevators aren't working. The power in the building is out."

Jay spun around, panic flashing in his eyes for a heartbeat before he regained his composure. "All right, stairs it is, then. I'll take a few of you with me to the top and work our way down. The rest of you start at the bottom and meet us in the middle."

Kayla's hand immediately shot up. "I'll go to the top; I don't have a problem with stairs."

Jay nodded and looked around—no one else seemed eager at the prospect. He sighed and named two people, pointing at them as he did so, then at Joel. "And you. The rest of you, you know what to do."

Joel swore to himself at the thought of how sore his legs were going to be but silently made his way to the stairs with the other four. They began the ascent, the spiral of stairs seemingly going up forever above them.

Each floor they passed was marked with numbers and names above the entrance, though none of them seemed relevant to their search. They passed MARKETING, FINANCE, IT, HUMAN RESOURCES, with several floors dedicated to each and more departments yet to come.

He had no idea how long it took for them to finally reach the top floor, but by the time they did, all of them were panting. They collapsed, sitting against the wall in the stairwell, the label above the doorway reading ADMINISTRATION. Jay silently reached into his bag and began passing out bottles of water and, strangely, markers. After several minutes of recovery, Jay stood up first, propping himself against the wall for a second before saying, "All right, that was rough. But now we're here, so let's get to work. Once you finish with a room, mark an X on the door and close it so we don't retread ground." He then disappeared through the entryway.

Joel, along with everyone else, slowly stood up and moved into the main part of the floor. Hallways webbed out from the space, offices and conference rooms lining both sides of all of them. Joel made his way toward the perimeter of the floor, and, once there, entered the first room he came across. The moment he looked inside he realized the monumentality of their task. The office's walls were lined with filing cabinets, and there were papers strewn across the entirety of the room.

Just as he began scouring through the files, he heard a knock on the door behind him. He spun around to see Kayla in the doorway. She smiled, then said, "I figured I might come help you; maybe we can keep each other company so we don't get lost in the papers."

"Yeah, I would really appreciate that. Thanks." Joel didn't vocalize it to her, but he was glad she was there. Her optimism and friendliness were keeping him grounded and, even if momentarily, happy. She nodded cheerfully and joined him, both scanning the library of documents as quickly as they could.

Every paper he glanced at was less interesting than the last—tax forms, corporate emails, administrative documents. Nothing at all pertaining to experimentation, and especially not to the sirens. Within fifteen minutes, the two of them had worked their way through the entire room's contents. They exited the room, and before moving on, Joel put a large *X* on the door with the marker Jay had provided.

As they entered the next room, they stopped as they looked toward the other side. The window was completely shattered, as if . . . Joel shook his head, clearing the dark thought, before continuing the search. Kayla continued standing still for a moment, disturbed, appearing to have reached the same conclusion about the situation that he had. She started to say something, but stopped herself and simply continued working in silence.

Several hours passed in a blur, time seemingly ticking slower by the minute. The group had progressed down several floors, yet none of them had uncovered any pertinent information. They had found many signs of the sirens in the chaos that ensued, but no information. None of it even seemed related to experimentation of any kind—all the documents Joel skimmed seemed normal, nonconfidential, and entirely unrelated to the sirens.

Their progress was interrupted by a faint yell across the building, the words unintelligible. Joel and Kayla glanced at each other, silently confirming what they heard, before Joel slowly made his way to the door and, poking his head into the hallway, listened for other disturbances. He didn't hear any other yells, but he did hear activity down the hall. Kayla popped up behind him, saying, "We should go check, make sure everything is OK." Joel nodded before walking down the hall, Kayla close behind.

As they got closer to the commotion, they saw several people gathered around a particular room, peering inside. Joel and Kayla glanced at each other, concerned, before closing the rest of the distance and joining the group. He nudged someone at the back of the group, asking, "What's going on?"

"They found someone still in one of the rooms, holed up in a closet, practically dead."

Before Joel responded, he heard Jay yell from behind them, "Why are you all standing around? What's wrong?"

The group parted, revealing a short, blonde woman, standing inside the room with a glazed look in her eye. Several people from the group were next to her, helping her stand. One of them was attempting to give her a bottle of water, but she was unresponsive.

As Jay's eyes landed on her, his face was nearly expressionless, but he abruptly stopped walking and even took a step back from the door. He exhaled slowly and then, without peering back into the room, called out, "Get her some food and water. I am going downstairs to bring in more help so she can get out of here—we need to get her back to base."

Joel looked at the woman, trying to see what caused Jay

to react like that, but she seemed normal other than her exhaustion. He looked back toward Jay, but he was already disappearing around a corner, presumably making his way downstairs.

Kayla weaved her way through the people and into the room, quietly saying something to the woman while guiding her into a chair. Joel stood outside the room, puzzled by Jay's behavior. He shook his head before squeezing into the room as well and approaching the woman. She seemed more aware now, taking small sips from a water bottle and looking at Kayla, who was speaking.

". . . group, not too far from here. You are going to be safe now. We are going to have some people take you there, where you can stay and recover."

The woman nodded slowly, shaking slightly. Joel quietly asked, "How long have you been here? What happened?"

She looked up at Joel, her mouth opened as if to speak, but no sounds came out. After a few moments she tried again, saying, "Two days. I was found by some people, and they brought me here. I heard them arguing . . . they said . . ." Her statement drifted off as she put her head down in her hands, crying. "I hid from them and didn't move. They left eventually."

Kayla quickly stepped in, saying, "Don't worry about that, just relax. You are going to be fine now." The woman nodded, still sobbing quietly. By this point most of the people had dissipated, going back to work. Just Kayla, Joel, and a couple of others remained in the room, watching after her.

A few moments later, a new person appeared in the doorway, winded. He held up a hand as he caught his breath, before saying, "Jay sent me up. Supposed to take someone down with me to bring them back to base. That's her, I assume?" They confirmed, then he continued, "All right, one person come with me with some water and food for the walk back and to help her."

Someone volunteered, and the two of them gently helped her up, saying, "We're going to take the stairs nice and easy; we have plenty of time to get back. If you need any time to rest, just let us know."

The woman nodded and, turning to Kayla, quietly said, "Thank you."

Kayla smiled and waved goodbye as they exited the room to begin the journey back to base. Kayla sighed and, turning to Joel, said, "I feel bad for her. Stuck up here without food or water, not able to even move because of whoever was with her. I'm glad she is OK now, though."

Joel nodded, feeling uneasy about the situation, before saying, "Well, let's head back to where we left off. We still have a lot of work to do."

"All right, let's do it."

They walked out of the room and began moving back down the hall. They were interrupted after a moment as Jay popped out of a hall in front of them, looking concerned. As he turned and saw the two of them, he raised a hand in greeting. They stopped and Kayla asked, "What do you think? Is she going to be OK?"

Jay frowned as he responded, "She'll be fine physically, but I don't know how she is mentally. She was smart and brought headphones with her, but they don't work as well as earplugs. Matthias will probably have her sent down to the second location, where she can be totally protected while she recovers."

Joel studied Jay's expression for a moment. He seemed very calm, and he had a strange look on his face. Joel didn't say anything, unsure of what to think of his behavior, but Kayla voiced her concern, though with a different undertone. "Are you OK? You look like you're feeling sick."

Jay seemed taken aback for a moment before he regained composure and responded, "I'm fine. I just thought I recognized the woman we found, but it was someone different. I'm going to get back to work—I would advise you both to do the same. We have a lot to go." He turned and walked off, disappearing down a hallway. Joel and Kayla glanced at each other, shrugging, before making their way back to the room where they had left off.

After resuming their work for a while, Joel looked out the window, which provided him with a view of the evening sky. The sun was well on its way toward the horizon, and yet they remained in the building. Joel considered bringing this up with Jay, but trusted his judgment of the time for now.

An hour or so later, Joel heard Jay yell across the building, "Everyone, come to the stairs. Group meeting." Joel and Kayla quickly stopped their work and wound through the building toward his voice. A minute later, they and everyone else on the floor were gathered in one place, Jay at the front. His eyebrows were furrowed, seemingly deep in thought.

A moment later, he said, "We have a problem. We aren't close to being done, and the sun is already within a couple of hours of the horizon. If we leave right now, we might be able to make it back before nightfall. Or, we can stay here and finish our job, and then camp out for the night here. It won't be pleasant, but the sooner we get this information, the sooner we can use it to our advantage."

The group looked around at one another, muttering, before someone spoke up, saying, "Well, hang on, if we might not be able to make it back in time anyway, why didn't you bring this up earlier?"

Jay stared at them, scowling. "I misjudged the time. It is what it is, now we have to work with what we have."

As the group talked among themselves, Joel considered both options. *Even if we left right now, we might not make it . . . Is that a risk that I want to take? But on the other hand, staying here is sure to expose us to more of the sound than being back at home base . . .*

Jay continued, "I should have spoken up earlier, but now I think our best option is to finish our job and stay the night here. Does everyone agree?"

His statement was met by uncertain mutters of agreement, to which Jay confidently nodded and said, "All right, I'll go downstairs and tell the other group. Remember to put your earplugs in before the sun goes down. Work as late as you want to, but no matter what, we will finish before we leave tomorrow morning."

As he concluded, he turned and quickly began descending the steps. Joel, deep in thought, continued staring at Jay until he disappeared to the lower floors. A few moments passed before Kayla quietly said, "Come on, might as well get back to work since we are staying." Joel nodded, then followed Kayla back to the room where they had left off.

They fruitlessly labored for another hour and a half before, looking out a window, Joel announced, "The sun is setting. Earplugs in." They both reached into their pockets and, after putting them in, resumed their search. As the room became darker, they each grabbed a flashlight from their bags, which, though not ideal, allowed them to continue, if more slowly.

As the minutes ticked by, Joel became more anxious as he awaited the sirens to begin. Since the power was already out in this building, there would be no warning as to when they would start. He looked over at Kayla, who seemed equally as nervous and, much like him, had practically stopped sifting through the papers in anticipation of the sirens.

Joel jumped, gasping when they began, their shrieks materializing from silence. Clenching his teeth, he attempted to continue his work. Kayla, on the other hand, sat down against the wall and put her head in her hands. Joel, noticing this, dropped down to her and, after getting her attention, asked, "What's wrong? Do you have them in?" He gestured at his ears as he said this.

Kayla nodded meekly, looking sick. Joel raised an eyebrow, prompting her to turn her head so he could see the vague shadow of it in her ear. She waved him on, pointing at the stacks of paper, and, to be heard over the sirens, loudly said, "Get back to work, I'll be fine."

He nodded, and, though still concerned, tried to resume his work. The moonlight now bathed the room in a soft silvery-white glow from the window, which, oddly, was bright enough to allow Joel to turn off his flashlight and still be able to read. Several minutes passed, and as he finished scouring the room for anything useful, he called out to Kayla, "I'm done here. I'm going to move on to the next room. Are you going to be OK?" Kayla nodded, and again waved him on.

After a moment of hesitation, he left the room, leaving the door open. As he walked, he became aware of the fact that the sirens were louder now, and the volume seemed to increase by the second. He entered the next room on the other side of the hall and, as this one was not facing outdoors with a window, had to get out his flashlight again to see. A few minutes passed, then his work was disturbed by a voice.

Joel felt a rush of panic pass through him, thinking he was experiencing what Kayla had described earlier, before he realized that it was *Kayla's* voice. He could barely hear it over the sirens now, the sounds seeming to resonate inside his head. He spun around and slowly approached the room where she was. She was standing up, loudly shouting something at the window, though in a kind tone—as if she was trying to make herself heard over the noises to someone.

"Cameron, is that you? Where have you been?"

Joel slowly stepped into the room, watching her closely—
she was silent now, then she nodded.

"Yes, of course I want to see you again. You know I do,
but . . ."

She took a small step toward the window, before recoil-
ing from it and grabbing her head. The moment she broke
eye contact with the window, her entire body tensed, and she
began screaming.

"Stop, stop, STOP!"

Joel, tense, slowly called out to her, "Kayla? Can you hear
me?" She turned around, tears slowly rolling down her face.
She appeared dazed, but the moment her eyes met Joel's, she
seemed to focus again.

"Joel, what's wrong with me? Are you real?"

He took a step toward her, his hands raised. "Yes, I'm
real. I'm the only person here except for you. Come out here,
away from the window."

She stood still, her lips trembling.

"But . . . I heard him. He was right there—" She turned
back to the window, and as she did, she appeared to relax.
"He is there. I . . . I can hear him. I can see him."

As she turned, Joel took another step forward toward
her, but he didn't make any dramatic motions, not wanting

her to panic and act irrationally. He responded as firmly as he could, "Kayla, focus. Look at me. There is nobody there. Don't listen to them."

Her head slowly and strenuously turned back to Joel. As she looked away from the window, she gasped for breath, her entire body tensing again. She made eye contact with him for a moment before her head snapped back to the window. She nodded slowly at something unheard, before responding, "You're right . . . I've been so worried about you this whole time. I already know Mom and Dad are safe, so . . . maybe this is how it's supposed to be. This . . . this is for the best."

She took another small step toward the window. Joel had crept forward, and as she finished her statement, he lunged for her, grabbing her arms and yanking her back from the window. She kicked at him, her gaze fixated on the brilliant moonlight beyond the window, and screamed, "Please! I need to go to him, he's right there!"

They struggled for a moment before one of Kayla's arms jerked out of his grip. Her gaze darted around the room for a moment before settling on an item on the desk next to them. She reached down with unnatural jerkiness, and before Joel realized what was happening, she began stabbing him ferociously with a pencil while trying to wriggle free of his grasp.

One of the stabs landed firmly, the tip of the pencil sinking into his arm. He yelled and instinctively jerked his arm back, releasing Kayla. She scrambled to get her footing before sprinting toward the window, shattering the glass as she dove through it.

CHAPTER EIGHT

It all came rushing back like a wave.
The grief that threatened to overwhelm.
Her voice called to me again though, this time more clearly.
I could hear her calling my name.
I had to follow her voice.
I turned my back to it all and followed her
voice back into the building.

Time seemed to slow—everything else disappeared except for the sound of his heartbeat and the cascade of emotions filling him. Joel took a step back, staring in disbelief at the shattered window. The shrieking of the sirens began fading, soon returning to the volume they had been just several minutes before. He stood, frozen in shock, unable to find the strength to move.

"Joel? What happened? Where is—"

Jay's voice echoed in his mind. Joel slowly turned, looking

at Jay, who was now standing in the hallway outside the door. He was staring past Joel toward the window, the blood draining from his face in sick realization. Jay was the reason they were still here. *He's the reason Kayla is gone.* As the thought entered Joel's mind, he became fixated on it—all his other emotions fueling his anger.

He slowly walked toward Jay, not saying a word. Jay didn't even seem to notice—his gaze was still fixed on the window, seemingly stuck in his own mind as well. As Joel reached Jay, he slammed his shoulder into him, causing Jay to stumble back against the wall of the hallway. Jay didn't fight back—he looked at Joel now, confusion and panic flashing across his face. Joel crossed the distance and put his arm against Jay's throat, pinning him to the wall. Joel, clenching his teeth, quietly said in a deadly calm, "You did this. You kept us here, for what? Did you want this to happen?"

Jay stammered for a moment before replying, glancing between Joel and the window. "No! I didn't know. Just trying . . . to do the right thing." He choked out the last words, his breath running out as Joel kept his arm pressed against his throat.

Joel didn't respond, his vision fading in and out from all the emotions overwhelming him. After a few moments, Joel jerkily lowered his arm and stepped back. Jay collapsed to the ground, gasping for breath. Joel slowly turned around and braced himself against the doorway, staring out through the broken window.

After a moment, Jay said, "Just . . . Just stay away from the windows, get into one of the inner rooms, stay with someone if you have to, shelter for the night. I . . . I'm going to go tell everyone else, we're done here."

Joel heard Jay's footsteps retreating from him. Joel covered his mouth with one hand, shutting his eyes, attempting to ground himself. The sirens, which had up until this point been entirely pushed aside in his mind, began wriggling their way back, filling the space left by the suppression of his emotions.

Joel jerked himself back from the door, looking away from the window, and began slowly wandering the desolate halls, searching for reprieve. Despite his earplugs and retreating farther into the building, the sirens were getting louder—piercing his thoughts, trying to find a way in. Joel stumbled into a pitch-black room, falling onto his knees as he gripped the sides of his head with his hands. *Why . . . Why . . . WHY?!*

"This is not a test. Evacuate immediately. There is nowhere else to go. Evacuate immediately. Evacuate immediately."

Joel scrambled up, crashing into the unseen wall of the dark room. He braced himself against it, tears rolling down his cheeks. The monotone voice of the alert was unnaturally clear, pushing all other thoughts out of his mind as he heard it.

"This message is broadcast at the request of the depart— This message—Evacuate—broadcast at the—civil—now . . ."

The voice broke, repeating random phrases in his head, morphing into new words.

"Go—outside—now—evacuate—test—flee— immediately . . ."

Joel stumbled back out into the dimly lit hall, excruciatingly bright moonlight streaming through every window, somehow reaching him even here. He ran down the hall, trying to escape the voice.

"Now—listen—go—outside—for—best—"

He turned a corner, running into the wall in his chaotic state, to see several people at the other end. Joel screamed out, "Help! Please, they . . ." His cry drifted off as he fell to the ground. The people quickly closed the distance and surrounded him, yelling things to one another that didn't reach Joel's mind. He felt their hands grab his arms, trying to pull him up.

"Please—with—Come—me—Joel—"

Joel's last bit of strength faltered, then he slipped into darkness, the words echoing around his mind.

———

Joel's consciousness faded in and out throughout the night, his dreams filled with flashes of grief, fragments of voices he couldn't quite hear, with the ever-present background of the sirens. Eventually, however, all the nightmarish sounds ceased, leaving him in a tenuous sleep that he soon woke from. He slowly opened his eyes, the daze from his sleep and trauma fading.

The room was filled with blissful silence, very dimly lit by the morning light trickling through the door's window. He had a rag over his forehead, and a half-empty bottle of water next to him. The room was lined with people, all sleeping with their heads resting on backpacks or other makeshift pillows. He slowly sat up, wincing, his head aching. He looked at the water bottle next to him and, after a moment of hesitation, quickly drank the rest of it. He stood up, legs shaking slightly, before quietly making his way to the door and out into the hall.

The hall was empty, save for the orange glow of light

at either end of the hall from unseen windows. Joel slowly walked, wandering through the building. He had no memory of how he got into the room last night, though he suspected he was carried there. Eventually he found himself at the perimeter of the building, the radiance of the morning sun streaming in through the line of windows in front of him. He stopped at one of the windows, basking in the warmth, looking out to the horizon.

From this height, the view was stunning. There were only a few skyscrapers blocking his line of sight, but otherwise he was above everything in the city, able to see beyond the city center and far out into the suburbs. He stood there for several minutes, enjoying the view, just as he had done with . . .

He cut the thought off, a lump forming in his throat. He let out a shaky breath, the events from last night crashing into the forefront of his mind. His thoughts were soon interrupted, however, by a voice calling from the end of the hallway, "Joel? Are you all right? We thought we lost you there for a minute last night."

Joel turned, facing the voice—Jay was standing near the end of the hall, with his shoulders slumped and bags under his eyes. Joel felt anger welling up as he saw him, but he quickly pushed it down. *There might be time for that later, but not now.*

He sighed and nodded, returning his gaze to the outdoors. Jay walked down the hall and stood in front of the window next to him, looking out as well.

"We are going to be leaving soon, now that the sun is up."

Joel didn't respond, staring wordlessly out the window. Jay frowned, eyebrows furrowed, before he continued, "I can't fix what happened, but I can get you all back to base." He then stepped away from the window and began walking down the hall, toward the room where everyone was sleeping.

After a moment, Joel turned to walk in the other direction. He needed to get his bag, which was left last night in the room where . . . Joel shook his head, pushing the thought down again, and continued searching for the room. After a couple of minutes, he stumbled upon it.

The door was still open, the shattered window letting in the golden glow of the morning. His bag was underneath the desk, also still open. Not looking at the window, he reached down and quickly snatched it. As he leaned forward, he saw a bloodied pencil lying on the ground. Joel clenched his teeth and quickly exited the room, shutting the door behind him. He retraced the path he took before, eventually approaching the room where they all had slept.

"Wake up, pack your things. Let's get the hell out of here."

Joel heard Jay's call as he approached the room, followed by several groans and the shuffling of people getting up. Joel waited outside in the hall for a couple of minutes until the group silently streamed out of the room, led by Jay. They all silently weaved through the halls until they got to the stairs, then began the long descent to the ground floor.

The journey back to the base passed by in a blur—Joel remained at the back of the group, following along in silence. Before he knew it, they were walking through the front doors of the home base. As the group dispersed, Jay approached Joel and said, "Come with me. Matthias will want to speak with you." Joel nodded and followed Jay into the elevator.

After a quick ride to the top floor, Jay motioned toward a chair in the lobby as he said, "Wait here. I am going to talk with him first." Joel sat in the chair, lost in his thoughts. Jay disappeared down the hall and into Matthias's room. Several minutes passed in silence before a commotion disturbed Joel's mind—he heard muted yelling from Matthias's room. Joel leaned back, peering down the hall with an eyebrow raised.

He couldn't hear any specific words, but the exchange was clearly heated on one side. Someone, whom he assumed was Jay, was practically screaming at the other, whose responses were entirely unheard. After a couple of minutes of this, the door at the end of the hall slammed open as Jay exited the room and walked back down the hall. As he passed Joel, he curtly said, "Your turn."

Joel's head followed him as he passed, wondering what had happened. He dispelled the thought for the moment and made his way toward Matthias's room. The door was still hanging open, but Joel knocked on the side of it anyway to announce his presence. Matthias sat inside, seemingly unperturbed. He smiled and beckoned Joel in, saying, "Come in, come in. Jay told me of some . . . disturbing events. I was hoping for you to give your account of what happened."

Joel sat in one of the chairs in front of the desk, looking down at the ground. "There's not much to say. What happened, happened."

Matthias frowned, clicking his pen. "Well, yes, but from what Jay told me, he arrived after, ah . . . After what he believes happened. You were the only person there to witness it."

Joel looked up at Matthias, meeting his eyes with a steely gaze. "The sirens got to Kayla. She jumped out the window. That's what happened."

Matthias sighed, setting his pen down and interlocking his fingers as he responded. "Joel, we need to work together here. I am very sorry for what you had to see and for what happened to her, but if there are any details that might help us in our understanding of the sirens, I believe you owe it to all of us to share that information."

One of Joel's eyes twitched briefly as he responded, "She heard and saw someone—she called him Cameron. I assume that's her brother. They got into her head and made her think her brother was outside the window." Before Matthias responded, Joel leaned forward and continued, his anger bubbling up again. ". . . Which would have never happened if we didn't stay in that building overnight. I don't suppose you know anything about that, do you?"

Matthias squinted his eyes, simply tilting his head at the accusation. "I'm afraid I don't know what you mean. From my understanding of the events, there wouldn't have been enough time for you all to get back here—"

Joel cut him off, saying, "We would have had enough time if Jay hadn't 'lost track of time.' In these circumstances, knowing full well what happens at night, he 'lost track of time'? If it hadn't been for that, Kayla would still be here!" He ended the sentence, his voice raised in a restrained yell.

Matthias thought for a moment, tapping his fingers together, before slowly responding, "These are stressful and trying times for all of us. No one is at fault for Kayla's loss— not me, not Jay, and not you. Among everything else that is happening, it isn't hard to imagine he got blinded in the moment by his mission. Someone else paid for his mistake with their life, and now he will carry that with him for the rest of his."

Joel leaned back again, biting his lip, before coldly, quietly saying, "Interesting that he was so focused on 'the mission,' considering we spent the entire day there and didn't find a shred of evidence that had anything to do with the sirens."

Matthias seemed taken aback for a moment before replying, "What are you implying? We had reliable information that that office might have held some clue about—"

Joel cut him off and, clenching his fists tightly, sharply said, "Don't lie to me, Matthias."

Matthias regarded him for a few moments, lips tightly shut, before he quietly asked, "They're getting to you too, aren't they?"

Joel looked up at him, the trauma of last night rushing back into his mind. Joel opened his mouth to respond, but didn't know what to say. Matthias nodded and continued, "I don't blame you for being frightened—especially if they are affecting how you behave during the day too. That is the reason you all were in that building—even with the mission being based on a rumor, with slim hopes of finding anything, we have to keep trying. We owe it to everyone around us, and to our families, to try to get to the bottom of this, even if we don't always come up on the winning side."

Joel nodded slowly, looking down at the ground. After several moments of silence, Matthias gave him a small understanding smile and continued, "Now, considering the effects all of this is having on you, I think it would be for the best if you took some time to rest, try to undo some of the damage that has already been done. And, at the request of your friend Emily—who spoke a good deal on your behalf yesterday—I would also like for you to go to the second location and see your family. I think it would do you some good."

Joel looked up at Matthias as he said this, his other feelings washing away at the thought. "Really? Where is it? When am I going?"

Matthias pondered for a second, flipping through several papers on his desk. He paused and frowned for a moment, looking underneath one of the stacks. He wrote something down on a notepad, then continued his search before landing on his target with a small "Ah, here it is."

His eyes glided down the page before stopping, as he said, "The most convenient time would be tomorrow, when the next supply run happens. You would be leaving at six p.m., help bring in the goods, then stay the night there with your family. How does that sound?"

Joel nodded slowly in response, prompting Matthias to quickly jot his name down on what Joel assumed was the schedule. Matthias put the paper aside and, as he set his pen down, said, "I apologize again for what you saw, and experienced, last night. I will have a word with Jay. Now please, try to rest before you head out. If you need anything, do let me know." He then gestured to the door, giving Joel a kind, if tired, smile.

"Thank you." Joel got up and made his way toward the door.

As Joel grabbed the handle, Matthias called out, "Oh, one last thing: Next time you see Emily, could you have her come see me? There is something I need to discuss with her." Joel nodded, prompting Matthias to smile and wave goodbye before he looked back down at his papers.

Joel left the room, closing the door behind him. He began walking down the hall and, moments later, was surprised by Emily standing in the lobby, looking nervous. She beckoned him forward and darted into the elevator. As Joel joined her, she pushed the button for the third floor and said, "We need to talk somewhere private. There is some weird stuff going on that I need to catch you up on."

Joel raised an eyebrow, saying, "Good to see you too." Emily glanced at him, a sheepish look on her face.

"Oh yeah, good to see you."

As the elevator dinged and the doors opened, Emily set the pace by briskly walking out and down the hall. Joel trotted to catch up to her, then the two of them wound their way through the building before entering a familiar room—the recording studio.

Joel closed the door behind them before walking toward the far end of the room, where Emily had taken a seat on her makeshift bed. As he slowly sat down on his makeshift bed at the adjacent wall, Emily said, "OK, so I told you I would find out what's going on, and I found a lead. I don't think anyone noticed. Before we get to that, though, what happened yesterday? You look like shit. No offense, I'm just worried."

Joel exhaled heavily, rubbing the side of his face with one hand. "Yeah, uh . . ." He looked at Emily, unsure of what to say. He didn't want to relive the memories, but at the same time he didn't want to worry Emily, who was looking more concerned by the second.

"I . . . Well, among other things, I'm getting worse.

Last night I heard the messages again—they were different though, not normal. The voice broke and started saying other things—it . . . it even said my name. But even more concerning than that, I think it's affecting me during the day, too."

The blood drained from her face as she listened. She slowly responded, "What do you mean, during the day? Do you still hear them?"

"No, I mean, like . . . emotionally. I feel less in control of myself. I don't know how to describe it. And I can hear them when I sleep now too—last night I was up and down all night with, like, fever dreams of the sirens and messages. Barely got any actual rest."

Emily bit her lip, thinking. She didn't seem to know how to respond. Joel, after a moment of silence, continued, "But anyway, Matthias has given me some time off, and he told me I could visit my family when the next supply run goes down there at six tomorrow, and that you were the one who convinced him of that. So . . . thank you. Seriously—if there is anything that will help me right now, it is seeing them again."

Emily nodded, giving a sad smile. "I'm glad he's seeing reason now, at least. When I was talking to him earlier, I didn't think he was going to let you go."

Joel frowned, quickly adding, "Speaking of, Matthias said he wanted to talk to you about something, so once we are done here you should go do that."

Emily's face paled again, her hand twitching toward her back pockets for a second. She slowly responded, "Yeah, I might know something about that. I'll sort that out later; first I need to catch you up on what I found. So, long story short, I stole a map from Matthias's office—"

Joel's mouth opened and he raised a hand, about to comment, but Emily glared at him and silenced the thought with a wave of her hand.

"The map showed three buildings, one being this one, one being the second location, and the third was an unknown place. So, I went looking for it, and I found it. Matthias *was* hiding something—they have a stash of working motorcycles!"

Emily paused after her exclamation, studying Joel's face for his reaction. Joel raised an eyebrow, confused. Emily sighed and continued, "Obviously we don't know what they are being used for, or how they got them working, but it's proof that they are hiding something. They are hiding the motorcycles, and they are hiding what they are using them for."

Joel's eyes widened as he sat in stunned silence for a

moment, before slowly responding, "We don't have any proof that there is some sort of . . . grand conspiracy here. What would any of their motivations even be? But it is interesting that they are hiding the motorcycles, though. What's the next step? Try to follow someone on one of them?"

Emily shook her head, thinking. "I'm not sure. I think for now I'll go deal with Matthias, then we can reconvene and go from there. You said you have until tomorrow at six p.m. before you get to go see your family, including the rest of today?"

After Joel nodded in confirmation, she continued, "Maybe we can go try to loot some sleeping pills for you to help block out the sirens at night, and while we are out, we can drop by the motorcycles and see what we can find. It's a good cover story, and will help you at the same time."

"Yeah, that sounds good."

Emily stood, taking a deep breath. "All right, I'm going to go talk with Matthias. You rest, sounds like you need it. Once I get back, we can head out—we should still have plenty of daylight to work with."

Emily briskly walked over to the door and opened it. She stopped in the doorway and, turning back to face him, called out across the room, "I don't know exactly what happened yesterday, but I know you weren't supposed to be out there all night. I'm glad you made it back all right." She then left, closing the door gently behind her.

Joel sighed and, closing his eyes, rested his head against the wall, trying to push the dark memories out of his mind.

CHAPTER NINE

I walked through those empty halls, following her voice.
It seemed to be only an echo—an echo of a memory.
But it was there. She was here, somewhere.
I heard other things, things I should have questioned,
But her voice made everything else fade away.
The halls were full of that blinding moonlight.

Emily took a deep breath as she exited the room, mentally preparing for the conversation ahead of her. *Did Matthias find out that I stole the map? What does he want from me?* She weaved back through the building, stopping by her room.

She took the folded map from her back pocket and stashed it far down in her bag before she turned and made her way to the elevator. After a quick ride, she exited into the lobby on the top floor.

Moments later, she found herself apprehensively knocking on the door to Matthias's office. From inside the room, she heard his quiet voice call out, "Come in!"

She steeled herself for a moment before entering the room, attempting to look casual. Matthias was already seated at the desk, all the papers on top perfectly arranged into stacks. *That's not a good sign.*

"Please come in, sit."

Emily slowly walked into the room and sat in one of the chairs, remaining tense. Matthias was regarding her with tired eyes; despite the circumstances, his silvery-gray hair was still perfectly combed, in stark contrast to the unkempt appearances of all the other survivors.

Matthias shuffled through some of the papers on his desk and grabbed one, setting it gently in front of him, before picking up a pen and saying, "There are a few matters I wish to discuss with you, to clear the air. I believe you have something of mine."

Emily met his eyes confidently, tilting her head. She opened her mouth to respond, but Matthias slowly held up a hand, halting her. He continued, "There is no point in me asking why, or asking what you know. Frankly, it doesn't matter. If you would like an explanation for anything, simply ask."

Emily kept her mouth tightly shut, unsure of what to say. Matthias nodded, sighing. "I'm not sure what I've done to earn such distrust from you, but I assure you that there are reasons for everything I do. The reason for the working vehicles is quite simple—we use them to carry information between here and the residential location. It is the simplest and fastest way to get important messages from here to there."

Emily cut in, quickly asking, "Why are you keeping it a secret, then?"

Matthias frowned as he responded, "If I told everybody we had working vehicles, they would all be stolen within the day, either to try to go to the second location and shirk their responsibilities here or, even worse, to leave the city, and you are well aware of how futile and dangerous that would be. It is in the best interest of everyone in this community—both those individuals who might do something foolish and all of us as a whole—to keep it hidden."

Emily leaned back, thinking. She couldn't deny the logic, even if she still didn't trust the motivation. She hesitated before asking her next question, wanting to be sure of her wording. "How are they working? All the ones stalled out in the road are dead, so unless you found a way to jump them . . ." Her question hung in the air, met only by silence for a moment as Matthias raised an eyebrow at her.

"As it happened, Jay was quite helpful in that regard. We would have been unable to do any of this without him—we owe much to him. He was quite an avid collector of vintage vehicles; it was his passion. He was the one who suggested putting his garage to use."

Emily frowned, almost wishing that he hadn't had an explanation. Matthias tapped his pen on the table, staring at her with a sad expression.

He continued, "Naturally, I will have to ask that you not share this information with others. I do hope at some point you will come to trust what we are doing here. That aside, I have a favor to ask of you."

Emily raised an eyebrow at Matthias in inquiry, prompting him to continue. "As you almost certainly know by now, Joel's mental health is . . . deteriorating. I worry for him, and I'd imagine you worry for him more than I do. I have him down on my schedule to go visit his family tomorrow evening—I think it would be good for him if you also went. I don't know if you are also struggling as he is, but I imagine no matter the case, it would also be good for you to get some time off from this chaos."

Emily slowly nodded, frowning as Joel's plight entered her mind. "I think it would do him a lot of good to get away from all this and recover."

"Shall I write you down to go with them, then?"

Emily nodded, pursing her lips in thought. Matthias clicked his pen and jotted her name down on the schedule. "Good, very good. The group will leave tomorrow, at six p.m. That is all that I wished to discuss with you—I won't take up any more of your time." He gave her a polite smile and gestured toward the door.

Emily slowly stood before quickly turning and making her way to the door. As she opened it, she quietly said "Thank you" before walking out and closing the door behind her.

Her mind whirred at the conversation, her suspicions conflicting with what Matthias had said. *He seems genuinely concerned for Joel, and for the well-being of all of us here . . . but I still don't want to trust him. There are too many shady things at play for me to just let it go.* She slowly made her way back to the recording studio, deep in thought.

———

Joel jumped as Emily entered the room. He had been zoned out, staring mindlessly at the wall ahead of him for the duration of the time Emily was gone. He cleared his throat before asking, "How did it go?"

Emily closed the door before pacing the room and

responding, "I'm not sure. He knows I took the map but didn't seem to care. He had, and has had, logical answers to all my questions." She turned on a dime and briskly walked toward Joel and, as she firmly grabbed his hands and yanked him up, said, "Come on, we've got things to do."

Joel stammered, beginning to object to her forceful tugging before he simply sighed and went along with her, quickly snatching his bag. Emily continued as they exited the room, "First order of business is getting you something to help you sleep. Then—"

Joel interjected, asking, "Wouldn't the supply rooms have something . . ."

Emily glared at him, causing his statement to drift off. She continued, "Even if they do, we need an excuse to get out of the building for our own purposes. Even though Matthias says the motorcycles are for carrying messages, I still think they deserve a second look."

After stopping by Emily's room for her to grab her pack, they quickly found themselves at the elevator and, after a short ride down, approaching the front doors. The two guards at the front stood at the ready, but seemed to recognize Emily. They didn't say anything as Joel and Emily walked past.

As they broke out into the afternoon sun, Joel shielded his eyes for a moment until they adjusted. Emily took a sharp left and began walking briskly down the street. Joel trotted to catch up to her, remarking, "You seem to know where you are going."

"Yeah, I know the general direction of where . . . well, you know where. We will talk about it once we get farther away from base. We can look for a grocery store or whatever along the way to get your sleeping pills."

Joel followed her, quickly losing track of where they were. At several points during their travel, Emily checked her watch against the sun, keeping close track of the time.

It was a very fancy, old-fashioned wristwatch; though he hadn't known Emily for long, it didn't strike him as something she would wear. Curious, he asked, "What's the story behind the watch?"

Emily glanced sideways at him, her hair bobbing back and forth as she walked. "What do you mean? Like, where I got it?"

"Well, you just didn't strike me as the type of person to own an expensive-looking fifty-year-old watch, so I figured there must be some story behind it."

Emily raised an eyebrow, giving him a small smile. "Well, you're right, I'm definitely not the type of person that would normally have one. It was my dad's."

Joel tilted his head thoughtfully, responding, "I've never

heard you mention him before. I take it he doesn't live in the city?"

Emily looked away, sighing. "Not anymore. He passed a few years back. Had some health issues."

Joel glanced at Emily, frowning. "I'm sorry to hear that."

"Yeah, well . . . we knew it was coming for a long time before it happened, so I had some time to . . . prepare. What about your dad? You don't talk about him much either."

Joel frowned, a flurry of emotions passing through his head. "I haven't seen him in years. He's not, like . . . *gone*, but he did leave. Ran off right after my mom had my sister, never figured out why. Mom certainly didn't want to talk about it at the time and she still doesn't now."

They walked in silence for a few minutes before Emily, clearing her throat, pointed ahead of them and quietly said, "That'll work."

She was pointing toward a large supermarket down a side road, which was attached to a small drive-in area that was labeled PHARMACY. Joel nodded in agreement before the two of them turned off the road and began walking toward their destination.

A couple of minutes later, they found themselves in the parking lot of the grocery store, sizing it up. Joel spoke first, quietly saying, "Looks like the pharmacy doesn't have an entrance from the outside. We will have to go through the main section to get there."

Emily nodded, voicing their shared concern: "Let's just hope we don't have another Jeremy situation. Quick mission, in and out. Just in case, you still have that gun with you, right?"

Joel raised an eyebrow and quickly slipped the bag off his shoulder, shuffling through the contents for a moment before seeing it where Emily had returned it after the second night. He exhaled heavily before replying, "Yeah, it's still here. Let's hope we won't need it."

As they approached the building, Joel almost ran directly into the front doors, instinctively expecting them to slide open automatically. He glanced at Emily sheepishly, shrugging. Emily gave him an amused and slightly concerned look before prying the doors open manually.

The sunlight that streamed in through the front doors of the store quickly faded into darkness, illuminating only a small part of the linoleum floor and the back of a few checkout lines. Joel and Emily glanced at each other before reaching into their bags and grabbing their flashlights.

They slowly progressed into the building, inspecting everything as they went. The building appeared lifeless—every aisle they peered down was devoid of people, though the contents of the store itself were in chaos. Much of the store had been looted already, but what groceries remained were scattered across the floor in varying conditions.

As they made their way through the store, a foul smell penetrated the air. Emily gagged and covered her nose, Joel soon doing the same. After a quick scan with his flashlight, Joel saw the meat market in front of them—with the power cut to the building, the raw meat was rotting and putrid. They gave the section a wide berth as they crossed the rest of the distance to the pharmacy unimpeded.

In front of the pharmacy were several aisles of over-the-counter medications, where Joel assumed the sleeping pills were. He started to make his way down one of them before Emily called out in a hushed voice, "What are you doing?"

Joel looked back at Emily, an eyebrow raised. "Getting what we came here for?"

She rolled her eyes, then pointed her flashlight toward the counter of the pharmacy, which was firmly sealed by metal shutters. "That's where the good stuff is. Do you want to be able to actually get some sleep, or just feel a bit more tired than usual?"

"Uhh, the first option, I guess."

"Right, then let's get back there."

Emily cautiously made her way to the door of the pharmacy and, without a moment of hesitation, firmly tugged on the handle to open it. The door didn't budge. Joel quietly remarked, "I don't know what you were expecting."

Emily glared at him before reaching into her pocket and producing her pocketknife. She flipped open the thin blade and, sticking it into the lock, began to gingerly pivot it back and forth. Joel's eyes widened as he watched. "You can pick locks?" he asked.

"I haven't done it in a while, but yes."

Emily swore under her breath after a minute of fidgeting with the lock. "This would be easier with a pick set, but I don't happen to have one handy . . ."

Joel became restless as he waited. He turned from the door and scanned their surroundings with his flashlight. The store was still silent and empty, the pervasive smell of the meat the only thing intrusive to Joel's mind.

The meat market was still clearly visible from where they were, though now they were able to see behind the counter and partially into the butcher's area. Something on the floor caught his eye, but he couldn't make out what it was.

Joel slowly walked away from the pharmacy, toward the butcher's room. He quietly called back to Emily, "Keep at it, I'm going to go check something." Emily muttered in response, not looking away from her work.

Joel covered his nose again as he crept toward the meat market, keeping his flashlight fixed on the unknown object. It was sticking out from the butcher's area, most of it hidden in the rest of the room.

As he approached the room, he stopped in sick realization—it was a hand, greenish-blue from decomposition, lying in a dried pool of blood.

He gagged at the smell, closing his eyes for a moment as he bent over, hands on his knees, steeling himself. He slowly turned the corner, covering his mouth and stepping back as he observed what was in the room.

Corpses lined the room in various conditions: Some were several days old, with their skin hanging loosely from their limbs, their features unrecognizable, while others seemed *newer,* their skin tight and ashen, their hands and feet purple from pooling blood. Every body had a single gunshot wound in the head.

Joel turned from the gruesome sight, closing his eyes as he tried not to vomit. He ran back toward Emily, calling out in a strained voice, "Emily, we need to get the hell out of here."

Emily glanced back at him, slowly straightening as she saw his pale face. "What happened? Why?"

Joel grabbed her by the shoulder, firmly pulling her away from the door. "There's bodies, there is a pile of . . . of bodies."

Emily resisted for a moment, her eyes studying his face in concern. "What do you mean, bodies? Like, human?"

Joel let his voice rise as panic began to overtake him. "Yes, bodies! There was a damn massacre here, we need to get—" Joel's eyes widened as his gaze moved from Emily to behind her. The pharmacy door was opening slowly.

Joel yanked Emily, pulling her to his side and turning her around. She started to object before she saw the wide-open door of the pharmacy. They couldn't see anything inside the pitch-black room, and no sounds emerged from the darkness either.

They slowly stepped back from the door, unsure of what to make of it, before a voice rang out from the room. "What do you want?" A towering, lanky man emerged from the darkness, a pharmaceutical white coat over his shoulders. He had very short blond hair and uneven stubble across his face. He was holding a gun in one hand, gripping it so tightly that his fingers and knuckles were white.

Joel and Emily both raised their hands, not moving. Emily slowly said, "He needs medication—he has insomnia. We need some sort of sleeping pill, anything strong." Joel glanced sideways at her as she said this, raising an eyebrow at the lie.

The man turned his gaze between the two of them, not raising his gun. After a moment, he turned and disappeared back into the pharmacy. Joel and Emily glanced at each other, not moving. A couple of minutes passed before he emerged again, holding a small baggie. He held it out, not moving from the doorway.

Joel and Emily cautiously approached the man until Emily was able to reach out and grab the baggie from him. He quietly but quickly said, "There are a few different types in there. I don't know what your prescription would normally be, so start with the minimum dosage and go from there. If you want to try different types, wait a few days for the old ones to clear your system. Got it?"

Emily and Joel slowly nodded, unsure of what to make of the situation. Joel hesitantly glanced down at the bag in Emily's hand, then back to the man, who was staring blankly at them, unmoving, his gun still held tightly in his hand. Joel swallowed and pushed down his apprehension to quietly respond, "Thank you. This will help a lot."

The man nodded, then he gestured with his gun toward the front end of the store. They both nodded in understanding before backing away from him. The man watched them with unblinking eyes until they got a good distance away, then he disappeared back into the pharmacy and firmly closed the door.

They both quickly crossed the rest of the distance in the store and, as they stepped back outside into the fresh air and warm sunlight, Joel exhaled heavily in relief. Emily was pale but otherwise seemed unperturbed. She handed him the medicine, commenting, "Could've gone worse. Let's get out of here."

She turned and began briskly walking away. Joel trotted after her and, after catching up, said, "Yeah, I think he was the one who . . . well, the one who killed all those people. They all had been shot."

Emily didn't respond, her breathing short. She shook her head, rubbing the side of her face. Joel raised an eyebrow, concerned, and asked, "Are you all right?"

Emily glanced at him, seemingly stuck in thought, before she sighed and responded, "No. We keep having close calls."

Joel frowned, replying, "I don't think he would have shot us—it was just a threat."

Emily glanced at him, saying, "Didn't you *just* say that you thought he was the one who killed all those people?"

Joel's cheeks reddened for a moment. "Well, yes, but the difference is that we got what we needed and left. We don't know what the situation with all those others was—maybe they just wanted to stick around to live off what remained of the groceries and refused to leave, or maybe they threatened him and tried to steal drugs."

"I guess, but it still was too close for comfort. I'm worried that eventually we will run out of luck."

Joel thought for a moment, considering her words. He slowly responded, "Well, we are still here, and that's all that matters for now. Let's focus on what we can do in the present, because nothing good will come from worrying about what could happen in the future." He wasn't even sure if he believed himself, but he hoped it would help alleviate Emily's anxieties.

Emily exhaled, nodding slowly. "Right, focus on the *now*. Keep moving." Joel wasn't sure if she was talking to herself or him, but either way she didn't say anything more after that.

They walked back toward the main road they had been on before Emily quietly said, "All right, follow me. The motorcycles aren't far from here." Joel nodded and let her take the lead as they walked, slowly progressing toward their destination.

After some time, Joel was caught off guard as Emily made a sharp turn down a small street. She stuck to the sidewalk, very close to the buildings. She quietly called back to Joel, "Be ready to hide if anyone comes riding by. We don't want to be caught out here."

Joel raised an eyebrow, asking in an equally hushed voice, "I thought Matthias knows that you know?"

"Well yeah, but he also asked me to not tell anybody, so I doubt he would be happy if he knew I was showing somebody exactly where they were later that same day."

They slowly crept down the street, passing a good number of buildings, before they approached the entrance to a parking garage. Emily quietly said, "They are all the way at the top, so let's just take the stairs. Last time I did a loop of every floor, so luckily we don't have to do that again."

They made their way to the stairs and began slowly climbing them. Joel looked at Emily as she walked, mind whirring with curiosity about her past. He hesitated for a moment, not wanting to intrude, but asked, "So, where did you learn how to pick locks, anyway?"

Emily glanced back at him, mouth shut tightly for a few moments before she responded, "It's not a part of my life

I like to think about. In the years before my dad passed, I had to take care of him alone. I couldn't afford the meds he needed, so . . . I made do."

Joel thought for a moment, taken aback by her words. Emily sighed and continued, "I don't regret it, but I wish it hadn't happened—any of it."

Joel nodded, thinking, *I can't imagine what that must have been like for her.* He somberly replied, "I'm sorry you had to go through all that."

"Yeah, well . . . it's behind me now. Like you said, focus on the present."

Joel nodded, unsure of how else to respond.

They finished trudging up the stairs and emerged on the top floor of the garage. Emily peered around for a moment and, after orienting herself, crept off toward where Joel assumed the motorcycles were. He followed, attempting to be stealthy despite the fact they hadn't seen or heard anyone.

They passed several rows of abandoned cars before Emily slowed to a halt and held up her hand to stop Joel. They crouched behind a car at the end of a row.

Emily slowly peered out from behind the car into the row—Joel couldn't see what she saw, but her eyes widened, and her mouth opened as if to say something, but no sound came out.

Joel tapped Emily on the shoulder, asking, "What's wrong?"

"They're . . . but they were . . ."

Joel sighed and, abandoning the stealth, stood up and peered over the car. The row was completely empty, aside from the lines of abandoned cars parked on either side.

Joel glanced down at Emily, whose gaze was still stuck on the empty space. She stood as well before quietly saying, "They're gone. He moved them."

CHAPTER TEN

Her voice led me into a room, with a glass wall
facing toward the outside.
There was something happening outside,
but I couldn't quite see clearly.
The moonlight. The shining, incandescent
moonlight. The voice. Her voice.
Before I could give another thought to the commotion outside,
Her voice echoed so clearly in my mind that
I could almost feel her breath on my ear.
"Come closer."

Emily let out a strained yell, rubbing her face with both her hands, before muttering, "I know he is up to something. He is so fancy with his excuses and cover-ups, but I know there is something happening here." She sighed and sat down, her back against one of the cars.

Joel frowned and, walking over, sat down next to her. He responded, "Couldn't it just be that since you know where they are, he needed to move them, anyway? It wouldn't really make sense for him to take your word for it that you wouldn't tell anyone. Case in point—" He gestured toward the two of them, raising an eyebrow.

Emily glared at him, causing Joel to raise his hands and quietly say, "Just playing devil's advocate."

Emily shook her head, exhaling. She thought for a moment before saying, "There's still another avenue we can explore. Chris said he saw Matthias leave his—"

Joel raised an eyebrow, interrupting. "Chris? Who's Chris?"

Emily waved her hand, continuing, "Not important, take my word for it. Anyway, Chris said that Matthias leaves at night and doesn't sleep in his room. I might not be suspicious otherwise, but he has a makeshift bed front and center in his room, which brings up a lot of questions."

Joel frowned. "So . . . what's the play, then?"

"I don't know. If I make sure I'm on the top floor when the sun goes down and the power goes out, I can see if Matthias leaves his room—and if he does, I can try to follow him."

Joel thought for a moment, considering objecting to her plan, before simply sighing and nodding. *I won't be able to convince her to stop prying—I just hope that she doesn't get herself into trouble in the process.*

Emily suddenly bounced up, seemingly rejuvenated, and held her hand out to help Joel up. Joel took it and, once up, Emily let go and walked away, setting a brisk pace. She called out behind her, "Come on, there's still plenty of day left. If we are going to find out, let's do it tonight. If we come up short, I'll let it go."

Joel started after her and, after catching up, asked, "So, where are we going now?"

They reached the stairwell, and as Emily opened the door, she glanced back at Joel and replied, "To talk to Chris again. He is going to be the key to make this work." They descended the stairs and began the journey back to the base.

After a while, a faint, growing noise cut through Joel's mind. Before he had time to wonder about it, Emily grabbed his arm and, dashing to the side of the road, yanked him with her. Joel let out a short exclamation, asking, "What are you doing?" She dragged him into an alley, off the street.

"Shh! Quiet—listen. It's a motorcycle."

Joel nodded and strained his ears—the sound was definitely getting closer. Joel attempted to peek around the corner of the building, but Emily sharply tugged his arm, shaking her head.

A few moments passed before the sounds, reaching their

peak, culminated in three motorcycles soaring past, each one close behind the other. Catching a flash of each person as they rode by, Joel widened his eyes in recognition. He quietly said, "I saw Jay on the back of one of those."

Emily glanced at him, replying, "Jay? The guy who led us back to the community?"

"Yeah. He led a mission I was on yesterday. He . . . well, he messed some things up. Matthias said he was going to 'have a talk' with him. I wonder how that went."

Emily frowned. "'Messed some things up'? How so?"

Joel exhaled, rubbing his eyes with one hand. "Long story short, he ended up getting us stuck out in the city overnight instead of getting us back to base. I don't really want to talk about it."

Emily nodded, looking concerned, but didn't press the subject. She quietly said, "At least we know they still have the motorcycles somewhere out there. Could be from anywhere, though."

Joel nodded and, following Emily, they entered the road again and continued their journey back.

By the time they turned the final corner and saw their destination at the end of the road, they both were drained. They crossed the rest of the distance and trudged through the front doors.

The lobby was mostly empty aside from the guards at the front door and a few people standing by the elevator. Joel quietly remarked to Emily, "Pretty empty in here during the day."

Emily looked around the lobby for a moment before shrugging and replying, "I assume most of the people are out on supply runs." They stopped behind the people in front of the elevator, waiting. A few moments later the elevator dinged pleasantly, opening to let several people out before they all packed in.

Emily leaned forward and pressed the button for the top floor before she joined Joel near the back of the elevator. They waited for the elevator to stop and let other people out on several floors before they arrived at the top floor.

The door opened, revealing the normal group of guards in the lobby. As they walked forward, one of them called out, "What are you up here for?"

Emily frowned and opened her mouth to say something, but Joel quickly interjected, saying, "We are heading to the roof—to get some fresh air."

Emily glanced at him, raising an eyebrow. The guards looked at each other before one shrugged and responded, "Fine, just don't be long."

Joel nodded and led the way down the hall to the left. Emily, under her breath, said, "I probably would have been less polite, but nice job."

Joel didn't respond for a moment as he was thrown back to his experience on the roof with Kayla. He shook his head and responded, "So, where is this Chris guy's room?"

"Follow me."

Emily led him down the hall and they soon found themselves standing in front of a door. She knocked on it firmly before stepping back and waiting. A minute passed in silence—Joel glanced at Emily, an eyebrow raised, prompting her to step forward and knock again.

Emily tapped her foot in impatience before reaching into her back pocket and pulling out her pocketknife once more. Joel, seeing what she was about to, started to object before she muttered, "Watch the hall, make sure no one is coming." Joel sighed, conflicted, before turning and keeping watch as Emily attempted to pick the lock.

After a minute passed, Joel quietly remarked, "So, are you actually going to get it open this time?"

Emily scoffed, saying, "Give me thirty seconds and it's open."

Joel counted in his head, still peering down the hall in case anyone came down. As he reached twenty, Emily let out a quiet "Got it!" Joel turned and saw the door cracked open and Emily looking very pleased with herself. She slowly pushed the door all the way open and led the way in.

The room was entirely empty—Joel hadn't seen what the room was like when Emily had been here the first time, but he imagined there was supposed to be more in it than just the floor.

He closed the door behind them and, locking it, followed Emily into the middle of the room. She was peering around, a thoughtful and confused look on her face. Joel, after a few moments of silence, said, "What exactly was the plan if he was in here, just sleeping?"

Emily glanced at him, shrugging. "Not sure. I guess he would have had a rather rude awakening, but we have a mission at hand here." She paused and looked around the room again before slowly continuing, "It looks like he has been moved out. Maybe he got sent to the second location?"

Joel shrugged. *I haven't even met the guy; I don't know what she wants my input on.* "Well—Chris aside—this can work, right? If no one is supposed to be in this room, we could just . . . hide out here until nightfall."

Emily thought for a moment before nodding. "Yeah, my plan was pretty much for him to let us stay here anyway." Emily glanced down at her watch. "We have a couple hours to kill before sundown. Just make sure you are back downstairs before the power goes out."

Joel raised an eyebrow. "Why would I do that? We *just* finished talking about the plan."

Emily sighed and looked at him. She seemed to hesitate for a moment before saying, "I'm worried about you. Your . . . symptoms . . . are a lot worse than mine. It's good to be optimistic, but not at the cost of your health. The safest thing for you is to be back in the recording studio, where basically all the sound is blocked out."

Joel opened his mouth to argue, but the words caught in his throat as he considered what she had just said. "What about you, though? Just because I'm doing worse than you are doesn't mean you can write off the damage to yourself as less meaningful."

Emily shook her head, quickly replying, "I'm barely experiencing any effects at all—no voices, nothing affecting my thinking. We need to know if Matthias is up to something, so if one of us has to do it, it's definitely me."

Joel frowned, unhappy with the situation. Various concerns and anxieties bounced around his mind, cluttering his thoughts. He shook his head, taking a deep breath, before saying, "Follow me for a minute." He turned around and walked toward the door.

Emily remained standing in the middle of the room,

looking at him. She called out, "What? Why? We don't want to get caught back here."

Joel glanced back at her, responding, "I told them that we were going upstairs, so let's go upstairs."

Emily shrugged and followed him. Joel opened the door and, once they both were out in the hall, led the way around the perimeter of the building to the small staircase up to the roof. Climbing the few steps, he pushed the door open into the evening air.

The sun was still a fair bit from the horizon, but it was far enough down for the colors of the sky to be warmer and dimmer, and for the skyscrapers to cast shadows far behind them, leaving swathes of the city in darkness.

Emily, closing the door behind them, stood next to Joel and said, "So, why are we up here?"

"It helps clear my mind," Joel replied, staring off at the horizon. Emily let her gaze rest on him for a second, unsure of what to think, before she looked out as well.

Despite what he said, his thoughts only became more cluttered—his previous anxieties and concerns crashing against the experiences with Kayla as they rushed back into his mind. He bit his lip, trying to push it all down.

Emily glanced at him, and seeing his expression, frowned

in concern as she remarked, "I know you said you didn't want to talk about it, but . . . I think sometimes it's better to get it off your chest instead of letting it ball up."

Joel closed his eyes for a moment, gathering his thoughts, before he replied, "Yesterday I found a girl I knew from high school here. We recognized each other and got caught up a bit. It was really good to see a familiar face, even though I hadn't known her very well back in school. She was with me throughout the day, and helped give me a better perspective on all this."

Joel paused for a moment, staring blankly at the ground in front of him, before shaking his head and continuing, "Yesterday, when we got stuck out in the city for the night, she . . . gave in. She said she could hear—and see—her brother outside the building. And . . . she lost the fight against it. She jumped out of the window. I couldn't stop her."

Emily seemed taken aback, processing his words. Before she responded, Joel continued, feeling a lump form in his throat, "And the scary part is, she said that she heard the messages I'm hearing too. It's getting worse and worse, and I'm afraid that I might end up . . . like her. And I'm not sure if I'm more scared that it will happen before I see Ava and Mom again, or that it will happen after I've seen them, and they lose me just as fast as I found them again."

Emily grabbed his shoulder and turned him to face her. She was moved by his words, but she pushed it aside for a moment. She looked into his eyes and firmly said, "Listen to me. You aren't going to give in. We're going to figure out what's going on, tonight, and then we'll go from there. Tomorrow you'll go to the second location to see your family, and you'll be totally protected from the sirens underground where they are. Just stay down there until we figure out how to fix this."

Joel slowly nodded, exhaling. Emily continued, "Tonight you should just hunker down in that recording studio, ear-plugs in, sleeping pill in, and get through the night. With the stuff we got you, you'll be down for the night once they start working. You're going to be fine, all right?"

Joel nodded, more confidently this time. Emily released his shoulder and let her worry show on her face for a moment.

She continued, "OK. It's getting pretty close to nightfall, so let's get ready for it. I'm going to go back to Chris's room and wait until the power goes out before poking my head out; you go back to the recording studio and take that pill. Once the sun comes up and the power comes back on, I'll come down and wake you up."

"OK—sounds like a plan."

Emily nodded and promptly turned to walk back to the

stairs. Joel sighed, feeling somewhat better about the situation. He followed Emily, and closing the door behind them, made his way with her back to Chris's room.

As Emily walked into the room, she turned and said, "All right. Make sure to use those pills—I don't know what the effects will be like since you won't be able to hear the sirens much, but they will help you sleep regardless."

Joel nodded and responded, concerned, "Be safe tonight. Don't do anything risky."

"I'm just going to get the information and get back to the room. Easy as that." She paused for a moment, then added, "I hope you make it through the night all right."

"Yeah, me too."

They both stood in silence for a moment, looking concerned for each other, before Joel nodded and turned to leave. Emily waved goodbye, then softly closed the door. Joel made his way down the hallway, back to the elevator.

Entering the lobby, he expected the guards to ask him where Emily was, but they hardly seemed to notice his presence. He simply entered the elevator and rode it back down to the third floor. While on the elevator, he checked to make sure he had what he needed for the night.

After a moment, he found his earplugs still in his pocket

and the pills in his bag, alongside other supplies. The elevator dinged as the door opened to the third floor—Joel nodded to himself, satisfied, as he exited the elevator and began winding through the building to the empty, condemned area of the building where the recording studio was.

A minute later, Joel found himself opening the door to the empty studio. After closing it behind him and turning on the overhead lights, he crossed the room to his makeshift bed and, putting his back against the wall, slowly lowered himself down into a seated position.

He rummaged around his bag until he found the small bag of medicine. He shuffled through the different bottles before hesitantly picking one at random. He set the bottle beside him, along with a bottle of water.

Joel rested his back against the wall and closed his eyes. He didn't know how long it would be until the sun set, so he decided he would simply take one of the pills whenever the power went out. He sighed and waited for the night to begin.

———

Emily stood ready at the door, waiting anxiously for the power to go out. She glanced at her watch—it should happen any moment. The seconds ticked by in silence. Finally, the light above her flicked once—then twice—then it burned out.

Emily already had her earplugs in, but the cacophony of noise as the sirens began still made her jump. The overlapping screeching of the sirens blended together into a constant background of white noise, slowly drilling its way into her brain; yet, she seemed resilient to it so far.

Without hesitation, she cracked the door open and scanned the hall. It was empty—everyone should already be in their rooms. *Matthias included*. She quickly made her way down the hall, stopping before the corner. She peeked her head around, looking into the lobby—which was also empty.

She could see all the way down the building, including where Matthias's door was. From what Chris had told her, Matthias left his room sometime after the night had begun. She waited patiently, one eye around the corner of the wall, for him to emerge.

After some time, she began to lose hope that he would ever emerge. The sirens grated into her mind—they were the only thing occupying her thoughts other than the unchanging view of the hall ahead of her. Finally, however, she saw a door slowly swing open.

A figure emerged that she quickly recognized as Matthias, his silvery-gray hair shining in the moonlight streaming in from the windows. He closed the door behind him and began walking down the hall, in the opposite the direction of where Emily was.

Emily bit her lip, hesitating for a moment before quickly turning the corner and walking down the hall after him, sticking close to the wall. *As long as he doesn't turn around, this will be fine.* Matthias reached the end of the hallway and turned the corner, disappearing from her sight.

Emily sped up, walking as quickly as possible. As she approached the corner she stopped and peered around it—Matthias still had his back turned to her and was walking down the long hallway, his features illuminated in radiant silver moonlight as he passed each window. Emily turned the corner and followed him down the hall. She squinted her eyes, trying to make out any details.

Matthias didn't look to be carrying anything, nor was he in a particular rush—he was walking leisurely down the hall, unperturbed by the sirens. Emily didn't know what to make of either observation. Matthias disappeared behind the corner once more, continuing on the path around the perimeter of the building.

Emily quickened her pace, attempting to keep up. As she passed each window, she felt a strange chill run down her spine. She peeked around the next corner—to see nothing.

The hallway was entirely empty, all the doors closed. Emily frowned, scouring the hallway in confusion. *He must have gone into one of the rooms.*

She crept forward, scanning each door for any sign. She progressed a small way down the hall before something caught her eye—there was a light coming from underneath one of the doorframes. She pressed her ear against the door before realizing that, with the earplugs in, she wouldn't be able to hear anything anyway.

She lowered herself to the ground and attempted to see underneath the door, into the room. She couldn't see much through the thin crack—she assumed the light was the moonlight flowing through the window, but it seemed excruciatingly bright to her. She could see the bottom of shoes in the room, unmoving, as well as the shadow of a figure extending all the way back to the doorframe.

Emily strained but couldn't distinguish any more details. She gently raised herself from the ground and, counting the doors in the hall, quickly made a mental note of where the room was. She retreated from the hall, winding down the hallways to Chris's room.

She arrived back at the room unnoticed—she quickly opened the door and firmly shut it behind her. She sighed in relief, her tension mostly fading. *I'll go back to that room tomorrow, when no one should be in there.*

She was relieved to have finally gathered some sort of information on Matthias that wasn't a dead end. *I'm not even sure if I want to find something in that room tomorrow. I would finally know I'm right, but . . .* She shook her head and closed her eyes, preparing for the long night ahead of her.

———

Joel jumped as the lights above him flickered. *All right, here we go.* He quickly reached for the bottle of pills and, taking one out, quickly downed it with a small amount of water. He had no clue how long it would take to start working, but he just hoped it would be soon. He lay down on his makeshift bed, attempting to get comfortable.

A few moments later, the sirens began—Joel didn't hear them, deep inside the building in a recording studio, with earplugs in—but he felt them. Even without their shrieks reaching his ears, their familiar presence began prodding at his mind. He took a deep breath, attempting to ground himself.

He lay there for several minutes, not experiencing any effects of the sirens or the pills. Against his efforts to stay calm, he felt his heart begin racing in preparation for what he might experience. The room was completely dark and silent—and Joel tried to rationalize that thought to keep the effects at bay. *I am the only person in this room.*

Despite the fact that the room was well away from the exterior of the building, he thought he somehow saw moonlight shining beneath the door. After a few moments, he heard a new noise coming through the walls, muffled—but still present.

"This message is brought to you by—" The rest of the statement was cut off by the sound of static. The voice sounded less synthetic tonight. Joel kept his eyes tightly closed, his back to the center of the room.

"This message is brought—this message—brought—this—this—this—"

The words repeated in Joel's head, getting louder. *How is it getting louder? It can't be getting closer, so . . . it has to be in my head. All of it has to be in my head, but . . . what does that mean for me?* The voice was getting clearer and more human.

"Message—brought—Kayla—"

Joel's eyes snapped open. *Kayla?*

"Please can—you hear—hear—me now? I—"

Joel sat up and looked around the dark room. The voice was quieter now but seemed to surround him. Now its words were strung together more, and the voice sounded almost . . . *feminine?*

"Joel—are you—are you—there? Please, say—say—something."

Joel's eyes widened as he recognized the voice. He quickly shut his eyes and, lying back down, covered his ears with his hands. *This is happening too soon . . . I can't be that far gone already, can I?* The next words he heard were entirely human, tinged with sadness.

"Joel?" Kayla's voice cut through his mind, drowning out all other thoughts. *It's in my head, there is no one there.* Joel's heart began racing, a burst of adrenaline shooting through him as he struggled to ignore the voice.

"Please . . . it's just me. Just say something, anything."

Joel bit down hard on his lip, not saying a word.

"Why are you being like this? Don't you know it's me?" Kayla's voice was very quiet and trembled slightly. Joel exhaled shakily, attempting to stay in control. *It's not her, it's the sirens. It's just in my mind. She is not actually there.*

Her next words were whispered so closely that he could almost *feel* her breath as she spoke.

"I just want what's best for you—I want you to be happy. You know I do. We have to stick together, Joel."

Joel let out a strained yell and, quickly standing, spun around the empty room. He yelled, "Stop! You aren't Kayla. You aren't real."

There was a small pause before the reply came, her soft, smooth voice resonating in his head. "Then why are you talking to me?"

Joel blinked at the reply, asking himself that question too. After a prolonged silence, he heard her whisper again, answering his own question. "If you thought I wasn't real, you wouldn't be."

Joel shook his head, backing up against the wall. He began to feel the effects of the sleeping pill, even against his racing heart—the drowsiness began overtaking him. He replied, "Why are you doing this to me? Just leave me alone. Please . . . I can't go. I need to see Ava again. She needs me. I can't leave her just with Mom."

He felt his mind becoming more vulnerable; the sirens drilled into his mind at the same time the pill began making him less aware. He heard Kayla sigh softly before the next whisper cut through his soul.

"I bet you'll see her again before you come with me—but you know that you will have to come with me eventually, right? You know that your sister is safe, just like I knew my parents were safe. So I knew it was OK to go and I'm happy

190

that I did. And you'll be happy that you did too. It's for the best, Joel."

Joel slowly slid down the wall before lying on his side, his head back on his pillow. He felt his awareness fading as the pill took over. Just before he drifted off to sleep, he heard one last whisper, echoing in his mind.

"I promise, you'll be glad you listened. I wouldn't lie to you; you know I wouldn't."

Joel's last feeling before he faded away was a foreign, involuntary trust in her words.

CHAPTER ELEVEN

I stepped forward, feeling tears well up in my eyes.

I could see something else in the window.

My reflection, approaching nearer.

Something else.

Someone else.

I slowly whispered her name.

"Serena?"

Emily didn't immediately notice when the sirens finally ceased. Sitting on the cold, hard linoleum floor with nothing but the endless shrieking made it impossible to get any real rest—her head was throbbing, and her thoughts were blurred together and fuzzy.

The overhead lights above her flickered back on, blinding her momentarily as the darkness was washed away by the stark white fluorescence. Emily, snapped out of her daze, quickly covered her eyes with her hands, groaning. *Why didn't I take one of those sleeping pills before Joel left?*

After giving herself a few moments to gather her thoughts, she slowly stood, wincing as her stiff muscles resisted the movement. She braced against the wall for a moment, head spinning, before trudging to the door. She put her ear up against it to listen for activity, before realizing that she still had her earplugs in.

She shook her head and, removing the earplugs, put her ear to the door again. She heard quiet shuffling of movement and muffled voices down the hall. She swore to herself, *Why are people up already? It's barely been a minute since the day started.*

She sighed and put her back against the door, thinking, *If Matthias was in that room all night, he is probably wandering around the halls right now too. But . . . I need to check on Joel.* She stood in hesitation for a moment before, making up her mind and steeling herself, she turned around and opened the door.

There were several people walking down the hallway toward the lobby, facing away from her. She closed the door behind her and began confidently walking down the hall as well. After a few moments, she turned the corner and saw a group of people standing in front of the elevator door. *Confidence, Emily. Confidence.*

She quickly crossed the rest of the distance and joined the group, standing close to the back of it. After a few moments, one of the members turned and, seeing her, tapped on the shoulder of someone next to him. Soon after that, several of the people were staring at her. One of them spoke up and asked, "What are you doing?"

Emily met his eyes and, raising an eyebrow, sarcastically replied, "Going downstairs? Why else would I be waiting here?"

They all glanced at one another, unsure of how to respond. The elevator binged and, as the door opened, the group started packing in. Emily rolled her eyes at the ones confronting her and, walking past them, entered the elevator. She reached forward and pushed the button for the second floor.

The door closed and, after a lengthy ride with people getting on and off at practically every floor, she exited onto the second floor. *I'll bring Joel some food too—I bet he would appreciate it.*

She walked forward toward the section of the floor stock with food and supplies and, after a brief peek into the contents of the room, settled on a small variety of granola bars, a box of crackers, and, to her delight, a large jar of peanut butter.

She stuffed them into her bag and, walking back out into the hall, turned to go to the elevator. She stopped, though, swiveling to face the opposite direction down the hall.

Being a repurposed office building of some sort, the hallway just extended out into the rest of the floor. There was a woman stationed at the end of the hall, though, who was presumably a guard. Hesitating for a moment, Emily turned and began walking down the hall. *If there is a guard there, maybe there is something I shouldn't see back there too.*

As she approached the end of the hall, the guard held up a hand and said, "Can't come back here. Off-limits."

Emily stopped and, attempting to look confused, replied, "Oh, I was just looking for the water—isn't it back there?"

The woman shook her head, curtly responding, "Food and water are in the room behind you."

Emily raised an eyebrow, considering arguing further, but sighed and simply turned around, quietly muttering, "Thanks." *Always one step ahead of me. I'll come back to that later.* She walked down the hall again and rode the elevator back up to the third floor, making her way to the recording studio.

———

Joel's dreams were fraught with voices and shadows, all of which were familiar, but he couldn't quite recognize them. Something broke through the haze, however—a new voice.

It was clearer than the rest, as if it were closer. It got louder, and louder, until . . .

Joel snapped awake as Emily firmly shook his shoulder, saying, "Hey, wake up. I've got food." He groaned as he opened his eyes, his head pounding. Emily was standing over him, holding what appeared to be a jar of peanut butter in her hand. She was giving him a concerned look, and after a moment she asked, "You make it through the night all right?"

Joel slowly sat up, nodding in appreciation as Emily reached into her bag and handed him a bottle of water. "I guess. The sleeping pill put me down pretty fast, but it's still getting worse. I remember talking back to . . . the voices, without really knowing why I was doing it."

As Joel spoke, Emily sat down in front of him and put the jar of peanut butter and box of crackers between them. After he finished talking, Emily swore under her breath before responding, "Well, that should be the last night you are anywhere close to them. Today's the day, remember?"

Joel nodded, exhaling slowly as he thought. *Today's the day I'll be able to see Ava and Mom again.* He reached forward to get a peanut butter–laden cracker before responding. "Yeah, today's the day. We are leaving pretty late, though, so we've got some time to kill. Did you find anything last night?"

Emily nodded, swallowing a bite before responding.

"Yeah, maybe. Matthias left his room, like I thought he would. I followed him for a bit before he disappeared into a different room. I obviously didn't try to go in, but I know where it is. After we finish here, I'm going to go back up and try to get in."

Joel raised an eyebrow. "Why didn't you try right when you woke up?"

"There were a ton of people in the lobby heading downstairs, I couldn't exactly sneak past. Plus, I wanted to come down and make sure you'd made it through all right."

Joel didn't respond for a second, internally grateful, before sarcastically saying, "Honestly, with the lengths you have gone to, I'm surprised you didn't just knock the door down and confront him then and there."

Emily nodded thoughtfully before replying, "Now that you mention it, that would have been more convenient."

Joel looked up at her and quickly added, "Seriously, though, thank you. I wouldn't still be here without you."

Emily nodded, a small smile flashing across her face. "Yeah, well, like you said a while ago—we make a good team. We've got to have each other's backs and make sure we make it to the end of this madness."

Joel nodded in agreement before he reached for another cracker. He paused for a moment, frowning as he asked, "Speaking of that, how are you doing? Any . . . effects?"

Emily shook her head, also frowning. "No, still nothing. Just the normal, awful sounds and the headache that comes with it. At this point I think we can rule out the amount of exposure we've both had, but that brings up the question: What's the difference?"

"I don't know." Joel sighed, thinking. *The sirens try to draw people outside; if they have to learn how to do that for each person individually, then . . .* He slowly said, "Maybe there's something about you that makes it harder for them to learn."

Emily raised an eyebrow. "What do you mean?"

"Well, if we are talking about the sirens as being intelligent, and their goal is to get in our heads and make us listen to them . . . If they can't do it to you, then they haven't found a 'way in,' so to speak."

Emily slowly nodded. "I guess that makes sense. So then, what would be the 'way in'?"

"Well . . . with everyone we have run across so far, I think they use people who were close to the person. The guy we found in the hotel said he heard his kids, Kayla said she heard her brother, and now I hear Kayla. So . . ." Joel let the sentence hang, realizing what the conclusion of his statement would sound like. Emily quickly spoke up, however, finishing his thought for him. "So, I guess there is no one they can use against me."

Joel nodded, looking down at the floor. *I guess that's a*

silver lining, but it's still sad. They finished eating mostly in silence. Once both of them had their fill, Emily packed the remaining food into her bag before saying, "All right, here's the plan. We are going to go upstairs, right now, and get into that room."

Joel raised an eyebrow. "We're just going to waltz in there? I doubt they're going to let us roam around the top floor for no reason."

"We have a reason—we are both going to be leaving tonight, so it would make sense that we'd go talk to Matthias to get all the details before we leave, just in case there is anything we need to know. Then all we have to do is walk past the door instead of knocking."

Joel frowned, thinking. "I guess it's worth a shot." Emily nodded and stood up, stretching. Joel stood up as well, and followed Emily as she exited the room. They wound their way through the halls back to the lobby. After waiting for the elevator to come and allowing several people to get off, they rode it up to the top floor.

The door opened to a much different lobby than usual. There were two people stationed in front of each hallway, blocking them, as well as the usual group of people in front of the elevator. Almost immediately after they exited the elevator, one of them called out, "No visitors today."

Emily raised an eyebrow. "What do you mean? We need to talk to Matthias; we're heading to the second location tonight. We just wanted to make sure we know what to bring and all that."

The guard raised an eyebrow in return. "He is also preparing to go there tonight. He's going to be holed up for the rest of today making schedules and setting up a chain of command while he's gone, to make sure everything keeps running smoothly here."

Joel and Emily glanced at each other. Joel, under his breath, quietly said, "I didn't know he was coming with us. That's new, right?"

Emily gave a small nod to answer him, but addressed the guard again. "I'm sure he wouldn't mind taking three minutes to get us up to speed, just so we are prepared."

"I'll get you up to speed. Be down in the lobby at six this evening—bring nothing with you. You'll have to help us carry supplies. Any other questions?"

Joel bit his lip, feeling the tension rise with the guards. He quickly responded, "No, that just about does it. Thanks." He firmly grabbed Emily's arm and turned her around before she could add anything else, guiding her back into the elevator. He quietly said, "We aren't going to win that fight. We can try to come back later; maybe the guards will be more amiable."

Emily aggressively hit the button for the third floor before muttering, "So, he is coming *with* us now? What is his game?"

Joel glanced at her, hesitating before responding. "He hasn't been down there since we got here—maybe he is just doing a routine check? Or, maybe he just wants to make sure I find my family?"

"No offense, but I doubt he would go through the trouble of spending a whole day setting up for his absence just to guide you to them, instead of just letting the people there do it. Whatever the case, I don't trust him. We are so close to figuring something out; we need to get in that room before we leave."

"I really don't see how we are going to unless one of us stays behind or something." Joel said this half-heartedly, already having moved on from the thought, but Emily's eyes suddenly widened, and her hand flung out and hit Joel's arm.

"That's it! One of us stays behind, and we don't tell him until the last minute. You go see your family, and I ghost the whole thing. You make up some excuse as to why I'm gone and insist you go ahead, then I can sleuth my way upstairs again and go into that room while I know Matthias is gone. It's perfect."

The elevator dinged as the door opened. Joel waited until they squeezed through the people waiting on the other side before responding. "That could work, but that's taking a pretty big risk in a lot of different places. Even though you seem much more resilient to the sirens up until this point, it still can't be *good* to listen to them for extra days."

Emily frowned, thinking. Joel continued, "And that aside, what if Matthias finds out? What if you get caught trying to go to the room? I have to imagine Matthias will have left guards up there so people can't just go through his personal stuff while he is gone."

Emily raised a hand, stopping any further comments. She responded, "OK, it's not a perfect plan, but no plan will be. I have to take some risks to see this through—I won't be able to relax, or accept that everything is OK, until I know for certain that Matthias either is, or isn't, up to something big."

Emily grabbed his arm and pulled him to the side, into a room. Joel quickly realized it was her normal room. He raised an eyebrow, asking, "Why are we in here?"

"There's no point going all the way through the building to the recording studio when it's not night. We just need a place to talk."

Emily turned and sat on the edge of the large desk, and Joel sat in the chair at the other side of the room. He thought for a moment before responding to her earlier statement. "I won't try to stop you if you are set on doing this, but just be careful—especially if you do learn something dangerous. Let's say for a moment there is some grand conspiracy; there would almost certainly be a contingency plan if someone found out."

Emily reached into her back pocket and, pulling out her pocketknife, began mindlessly etching something into the desk as she thought. A few moments later, she responded, "Actually, tonight will be a good telling if that's the case—if there is something to hide, there is no way Matthias will be OK with you all leaving without me, right? If there *is* a conspiracy, he won't let the one person who is suspicious of him stay here while he leaves."

"That would make sense, yeah. Still, that means there is nothing we can do but wait. One way or another, we'll get some answers tonight."

"Yeah, I guess."

They made some small talk as the hours passed, but Joel got increasingly agitated as six p.m. approached. The minutes seemed to tick slower and slower the more aware he was that he was simply waiting for them to pass. Finally, however, Emily looked down at her watch and announced, "It's about time. You should head down to the front lobby."

Joel sighed, exhaling nervously. He felt a swirl of emotions in his mind, ranging from excitement to anxiety. "What's your strategy? You've had all day to think about it."

Emily nodded, replying, "I'll see you to the elevator, but I won't go farther than that. I don't want to risk being seen in the lobby with everyone else who is leaving. It would ruin the whole *she couldn't make it* bit."

"All right, then, let's go." Joel set his bag down, prompting Emily to raise an eyebrow. "They said to not take anything with me so I could help carry supplies, so I'm just leaving my bag here."

"Fair enough, I guess."

Joel turned and led the way to the door, Emily close behind. He tried to push down the nerves as he opened the door, preparing himself for the journey ahead. Very soon after they exited the room, though, he heard a call from down the hall.

"Ah, Joel, Emily, I was just coming to get you. It's time to go."

———

Matthias was standing in the hallway, halfway between the lobby and the room. Emily swore under her breath, but she quickly regained her composure. Matthias gestured them forward, prompting Joel to walk toward him. Emily remained, however, calling out, "One second, let me grab a bottle of water before we go."

Matthias responded, "Sure, we'll wait for you out here."

Joel glanced at Emily, raising an eyebrow in question, before crossing the distance to Matthias. Emily turned and entered the room again, a flurry of thoughts running through her head. *Shit! What are the odds of that? I should have known better than to leave the room at all.*

She quickly walked to Joel's bag and scoured through it before hesitantly placing her hand on the gun, still sitting near the bottom, unused since the second night.

She shook her head, pushing out the second thoughts, and stashed the gun in her waistband behind her back, concealing it with her shirt. She grabbed a bottle of water to cover for her lie, then headed toward the door.

———

As Joel walked down the hall, Matthias asked, "How are you feeling? Ready to see your family again?"

Joel nodded, smiling. "Yeah, I've been ready for a while now."

Matthias nodded, smiling in return. Joel heard the door reopen behind them, followed by Emily's quick footsteps. Once she caught up, he heard her say, "All right, I'm ready. Let's go."

"Very good, very good. We already have our supply bags

gathered in the lobby, so there will be no need to stop by the second floor. Just be ready to carry some things." Matthias said this as he turned, leading the way back to the elevator.

Joel hung back to quietly ask Emily, "Why did you go back in the room?"

"A contingency plan of my own. Don't worry about it."

Joel gave her a concerned look before shrugging and diverting his attention back to the hallway. They entered the elevator and, after a quick ride down, exited into a busy lobby.

Several people were standing around, most of whom Joel recognized as guards from the top floor. There was a sizable pile of backpacks and bags, all filled to the brim with unknown goods. Matthias walked to them and, after shouldering a backpack, picked up a bag in each of his hands. This prompted all the others to do the same.

Joel and Emily followed their example, grabbing as much as they could carry. After all the bags had been picked up, Matthias called out, "All right, let's get a move on. We should have plenty of time to get down there before nightfall—and for those of us returning to make it safely back—but we have to leave now."

Emily raised an eyebrow and, quickly crossing the distance to Matthias, asked, "What do you mean 'those of us returning'?"

Matthias glanced at her, seeming strained by the bags he was carrying. "As you have probably noticed, many of our party are normally stationed around the building. Most of them need to get back here before nightfall to make sure things stay running smoothly. In fact, this time around, I think only you, Joel, and I will be staying overnight at the second location."

Matthias turned and led the way outside. Emily glanced at Joel, scanning his face for a response. He shrugged, quietly saying, "Seems reasonable." Emily frowned but turned and followed Matthias without further comment. Joel followed as well, and in moments the group had left the building, wandering into the warm evening sun.

Matthias took a sharp right, presumably leading the group to where the motorcycles were now being stored. Matthias glanced back and called out, "Emily, Joel, come here. I want to go over some things with you before we get on our way."

They glanced at each other but crossed the distance to stand next to Matthias. He continued, saying, "Just to measure your expectations, once we get there you won't be able to see your family immediately. I will expect you both to bring in the supplies first before settling in. Our first priority has to be finishing our job so the rest can hurry back to base before nightfall."

Joel and Emily nodded, prompting Matthias to say, "Also, given the circumstances, I must inform you that we are, of course, going to be taking the motorcycles. It is a fair distance out from here, so it would be foolish to try to walk laden with all the bags. I assume by now you have told Joel about them, so I thought I should be candid about their usage."

Emily's cheeks reddened and she looked away. Joel quickly commented, "She might have mentioned them, but I thought nothing of it. They are there for a reason, so why argue?"

Matthias smiled, replying, "Yes, indeed. We should all be very thankful to Jay for providing those. Without them, we would have a much harder time making this setup work."

Emily frowned, replying, "Speaking of Jay, where has he been? I haven't seen him in a while, but I thought he was supposed to be in charge of organizing supply runs and whatnot."

Matthias sighed, frowning. "Ah, well, if you must know—he made a rather large mistake on the job and has been suffering from the consequences of it. I don't blame him for taking it hard, given the circumstances around what happened, but that kind of emotional vulnerability is exactly the sort of thing that leads to people being more profoundly affected by the sirens."

They fell into a brief silence before Joel, changing the topic, asked, "So, I should have asked this sooner, but I was wondering if I could stay longer than just a few days. If this place is entirely safe from the sirens, by being underground or whatever, I need that kind of immunity right now. My . . . symptoms . . . are getting worse by the day."

Matthias looked at Joel, concerned. "Yes, of course, think nothing of it. I was figuring it would be best you stay there anyway. I think you will be much happier, reunited with your family."

Joel smiled, nodding. He felt a lump form in his throat at the thought of seeing Ava again. *Just an hour or so longer.* Emily, seemingly deep in thought about something, asked, "What should we expect when we get there? Who should we talk to, to find Joel's family?"

"Well, you would talk to me, I suppose. Aside from attempting to make regular checkups on the second location, I also would like to give you and Joel a personal tour, and ensure you find your place."

Emily nodded, but her concerned look deepened at the response. They fell into silence again as they weaved through the city grid. Joel quickly lost track of where they were, despite not having been walking for more than fifteen minutes.

They soon turned into a small unremarkable alley, but

it was packed with a variety of motorcycles. Each one had a large box on the back of it and bars sticking out from the side. The members of the group began loading bags into the boxes and slinging bags over the bars.

Matthias set down his two bags, sighing in relief as his arms were allowed to rest, before picking up a small bucket on the ground. He quickly passed out keys to every member of the group—except Joel and Emily.

Emily quickly spoke up, saying, "Hey, you forgot us. I know how to ride a motorcycle."

Matthias glanced at her and, smiling, said, "Well, that's very good, but don't worry about it. Normally our extras don't know how to, so they simply ride with one of the others. Everyone already has an assigned vehicle; it will be simpler if you each hop onto the back of one. In fact, if you would go to one of those two"—he pointed to what looked like the two bulkiest motorcycles—"they have a bit more power to carry extra weight."

Emily opened her mouth to say something more, but Joel quickly said, "That will work fine, whatever gets us there faster."

Emily glanced at him, looking nervous. Joel shrugged, then made his way toward one of the large motorcycles. All he could think about was Ava. He knew how to ride a motorcycle too, but he just wanted to get there. *I'm not too proud to ride with someone else. What's her deal?*

Everyone began mounting their respective motorcycles, Joel climbing on behind the rider of his. He glanced at Emily, who was standing where she had been, glancing frantically between him and the motorcycle she was supposed to get on. He beckoned her forward, mouthing, "It's going to be OK."

Emily closed her eyes, exhaling heavily, before striding toward her motorcycle with a strange determination. Joel considered it for a moment before pushing it aside, focusing only on the thought of Ava.

One by one, all the riders started their engines and began to creep out of the alley. The ones Emily and Joel were on were at the very back of the group, but soon enough they also began slowly making their way out of the alley, the engines rumbling gently.

As they emerged onto the street and began riding into the distance, Joel closed his eyes for a moment, waves of emotion already rolling through his body. *This is it.*

CHAPTER TWELVE

She smiled and beckoned me closer.

I stepped closer and closer to the window.

Something was happening behind her, though,

outside of the window.

Things I couldn't quite make out.

Things I perhaps didn't want to see.

As though she read my mind, she whispered,

"Just look at me. It's all okay now."

She seemed to come into focus not in the reflection,

but outside the window itself.

She put her hand up against the glass, repeating,

"It's all going to be okay now."

I felt the weight lift from me—that terrible burden I had borne.

Tears blurred my vision as I pressed my hand

against hers through the glass.

Emily let out a shaky breath, closing her eyes. They had only been riding for several minutes, the rider of

Emily's motorcycle falling into place at the back of the group. Matthias had her cornered—he had covered almost every possible way of her going rogue. *Almost.*

She reached behind her, feeling the gun hidden in her waistband. *He can't know I have this. If I can get out of here without the rest of the group noticing, I can get back to base without any resistance, and I know Matthias will be gone.*

She hesitated, knowing there would be no going back if she did this. If she pulled the gun out and went through with this, she would potentially be exiling herself from the community forever. She would never be trusted, or accepted, again.

Biting her lip in indecision, she argued back and forth with herself. *If you do this, everything changes, one way or another. Is that a risk you want to take?* She shook her head, dispelling the hesitations.

I'm doing this for Joel. I don't trust Matthias, or this "second location." If I'm going to make a move, I have to do it now. I can't just play into his hand. Steeling herself, she slowly reached into her waistband and pulled out the handgun. *It's now or never.*

She reached over and knocked several bags off the side of the motorcycle. The rider slowed dramatically as the balance of the motorcycle shifted. Before she could change her mind, she shoved the gun firmly against the rider's side.

"Slow down. Now," she ordered as quietly as possible while still being heard over the engine.

The rider glanced back, opening his mouth to exclaim something, but his eyes widened, and the blood drained from his face as he saw the gun.

"Don't call for help. If you make a single sound, I shoot. Understood? Make a turn and start driving, not to where they are going. Away from anything."

Gripping the handlebars so tightly that his knuckles were white, the man nodded. After glancing for a moment at the group driving into the distance, he steered the motor-cycle into the nearest intersecting road that was pointing to another edge of the city.

They drove for several miles before she directed him into a nearby alleyway. She poked the gun hard into his back again, sharply saying, "Good. Get off."

The man slowly raised his hands from the handlebars and slid off the seat. Emily scooted forward, still pointing the gun at the man. "If you want to get back to base before sunset, start walking. You don't have much time to spare."

The man nodded again, mouth firmly closed.

Emily slowly drove down the alley, emerging out on a different road, parallel to the first one. She stashed the gun in her waistband before turning the motorcycle down the road toward the way they had come, and revving the engine, began flying back to the base.

———

Joel's thoughts, for the first time since this all began, were peaceful. They had been riding for some time now, cruising along the mostly empty sidewalks of the grid in a seemingly straight shot toward the edge of the city.

He sighed, his thoughts turning to Emily. He glanced back for a moment, wanting to give her a reassuring gesture of some kind, but he saw nothing. He glanced over his shoulder in the other direction, seeing nothing there as well. *I know they were behind us, so where are they?*

Joel frowned, opening his mouth to say something about it to the rider, before a thought entered his head. *She might have bailed to go back to the base. She was acting really twitchy and anxious, so it would make sense. Especially since she knows Matthias will be gone from the building. If that is her plan, I'd better not say anything.* He closed his mouth again, eyebrows furrowing in thought.

He suddenly began doubting his own trust of the situation.

If Emily was suspicious enough to ditch us, even knowing that she would be caught eventually, maybe I should be a bit more cautious as well. But . . . His mind turned to Ava again, all of his other thoughts washing away.

He smiled, a sense of bliss returning. *Why should I be cautious? I'm going to get to see Ava again. I can finally rest, knowing that she and Mom are safe.* He blinked, shaking his head for a moment to clear his mind. *No, I definitely should play it safe. I should have backed Emily up earlier.*

No, you were right to brush her off. She was trying to get in the way of you seeing Ava. She was just causing a scene. Joel closed his eyes, rubbing his forehead. *That doesn't even make sense—why would she want me to not see Ava? It's Matthias she doesn't trust, not some malicious will against me . . .*

His contemplation petered out as he realized the contradictory nature of his own thoughts. *Why am I arguing with myself? Why am I even blindly trusting Matthias in the first place? Emily and I have been uncovering shady things about him since day one. It doesn't even make sense for me to suddenly trust him unwaveringly, unless . . .*

Joel's eyes widened in revelation. *Unless they aren't my own thoughts.*

Emily slowly brought the motorcycle to a halt about a block away from the base. She stashed it in an alley, hoping no one would find it, before sprinting the rest of the distance toward the building. There were several people leaving as she approached it, but they quickly scattered when she barreled through them into the building, gripping the straps of her backpack tightly.

The guards on either side of the door called out to her, saying, "Hey, be careful! You could hurt somebody, running like—" She tuned them out as she firmly pushed the button multiple times to call the elevator. After a few moments, the elevator dinged pleasantly as the door opened. Emily rushed in and, pushing the button, rode it to the top floor.

The doors opened to a lobby scene similar to the one she was in that morning. There were two guards sitting in chairs, watching the elevator. The moment she emerged from the elevator, both of them turned their attention to her. One called out, "Hey, you aren't supposed to be up here. Matthias is gone for the evening."

Emily, furrowing her eyebrows and narrowing her eyes, reached behind her and pulled out the gun again. The two men in chairs jumped up, raising their hands. One of them quickly said, "Whoa, we aren't armed, we aren't going to do anything. Just relax."

Emily, stepping forward, gestured with the end of the gun toward the right hall, saying, "Anyone down there?"

They quickly shook their head, saying, "No, there's just us. Everyone else went with Matthias."

Emily nodded and began marching down the hall. She turned and pointed the gun back at them, calling out, "Don't follow me, don't get help. No one gets hurt as long as you just stay out of my way." They both nodded, prompting her to turn back around.

She sprinted down the hallways, past Matthias's room, heading toward the other room from the night before. Several moments later, she stood in front of the door she remembered. She tested the door, to find it locked. She let out a strained yell of frustration as she began firmly kicking the door below the lock, attempting to knock it down.

The door did not give way, however. She took a moment, stabilizing herself, before looking down at the knob. She quickly patted her back pocket, searching for her knife, before she realized she'd left it sitting on the office desk earlier that day.

She swore, sprinting back down the hallway. As she approached the guards, who were both standing beside one another, quietly whispering among themselves, she yelled, "Keys! Where are they?"

They both spun around, quickly raising their hands again. One of them replied, "What? What keys?"

"The master keys, Matthias's keys, whatever, I need the keys."

"I—I think he keeps them on him. He didn't give any of us keys to his office."

She raised the gun again, tilting her head.

Both of them started yelling at once, their voices jumbled together. "We swear! We don't have the keys; we can't get into his office either!"

She swore again and lowered the gun, thinking. She slid the backpack of unknown goods off her shoulder and quickly unzipped it, raising an eyebrow. Inside, resting on top of the pile of supplies, was a stack of long, ripped pieces of fabric. Both of her eyebrows flew up. *What on earth were they going to use all this for?* She pushed the question aside and pulled out several pieces, barking, "You two! Turn around, stand still, apart from each other. If either of you try anything, I will shoot, understand?"

They both nodded vigorously and turned around, arms at their sides. Emily slowly approached, keeping the gun firmly pressed against each one's back as she deftly tied the strips of fabric around his arms, and then legs. Once she was satisfied with her work, she quickly dashed to the elevator and mashed the button for the third floor.

While she was in the elevator, she hid the gun again. A few moments later, she exited onto the third floor and sprinted toward her room. Several people in the hall gave her a concerned look as she barreled past them, but she paid them no mind.

She entered her room and, after quickly snatching her pocketknife from the desk, stopped to search in the bottom of her bag for the map. Stashing both in her back pocket, she sprinted back to the elevator.

After a short ride back up, she gave a quick glance to make sure the pair of guards were still there, tied up. She ran past them and along the perimeter of the building. She deftly slid to her knees in front of the door and, pulling out her knife, began to pick the lock.

———

Joel's mind reeled from his insight. *Have I even been acting of my own will? If they can control my thoughts, or manipulate my emotions to such an extent that I start blindly ignoring the feelings that they don't want me to feel, what does that mean for me?*

The group of motorcycles turned down another road, stalling his thoughts as his balance shifted. He leaned forward, yelling over the sound of the air rushing past them and the engine roaring, "Hey! Have you been to the second location before?"

The rider nodded, not looking from the road. "Yeah, a few times. We make trips down here pretty often."

"What's it like? What should I expect?"

The rider tilted his head, thinking, before responding, "I'm not sure what you want me to say. It's just another place. This one is just safer than the other."

Joel frowned, unhappy with the response. "Where is it?"

"Right on the outskirts of the city center."

"I thought Matthias said that it's out in the suburbs, some sort of underground complex."

The rider was silent for a moment before responding. "The entrance is on the outskirts of the city; the place itself reaches into the suburbs."

Joel's mind began whirring. He felt as if he was trying to piece together a puzzle, but he had one piece missing. "Well, have you ever been inside?"

"Yeah, when we bring supplies in there. We're going to be there soon; you'll see for yourself."

They rode in silence for a few minutes, Joel's mind

becoming increasingly chaotic the more he thought about what was happening. *If the sirens are manipulating my emotions so that I go along with this plan . . . What does that even mean?*

They turned another corner, the edge of the city center visible as the skyscrapers and high-rises gave way to residential areas. The group of motorcycles began slowing, before stopping in front of a large high-rise at the very edge of the city, giving them a good view of the horizon and of the sprawling suburban areas extending out for miles.

Everyone began dismounting their vehicles, prompting Joel to do the same. He looked around him, raising an eyebrow. *This isn't what I expected.* Matthias called out from near the front of the group, "All right, everyone grab a few bags and let's get going. Joel, up front with me. I'll make sure you find your family."

Joel slowly approached Matthias and, gesturing toward the large building behind them, asked, "This is it? Doesn't look like an underground place."

Matthias smiled, saying, "Well, the entrance has to be aboveground, right?" He then frowned, asking, "Where is Emily? I don't see her."

Joel feigned surprise, turning and scanning the group.

Matthias held a finger up and, after counting, said, "We are missing a motorcycle. It seems they got lost along the way. Did anyone see what may have happened to them?"

All the members of the group glanced at one another, not saying anything.

Matthias sighed before calmly saying, "No matter, I'm quite sure she will turn up eventually."

He then turned and led the way up a small series of steps to the front door of the building. Joel followed soon after, with the rest of the group fanning out and following behind them.

———

Emily worked furiously on the lock for a few minutes, yelling in relief when it finally gave way. She stood and, not wasting a moment, put her knife back in her pocket and slowly opened the door.

The room was barren—it was entirely devoid of furniture, with the exception of what looked like a pulpit of some kind situated in the middle. Sitting on the pulpit were two stacks of papers, a small cup of pens, and a neatly bound journal.

The room was flooded with the orange glow of the evening sun, which Emily realized after a moment was because the windows weren't covered like they were in every other room. Only a glass pane sat in the window, leaving nothing to block the light from entering the room.

She slowly stepped forward to the pulpit, looking at its contents. One stack of paper was blank, but the other was filled front to back with scrawled, cramped writing. Each line was unrelated to the last, and she couldn't tell what any of it was supposed to be saying.

She reached toward the journal and, opening it, saw that the first page was much more organized and readable, despite being in the same handwriting. Her eyes drifted down and she began reading the text, which was written strangely, each line of text residing in the middle of the page.

I stepped back. Each heartbeat rang in my ears like
a drum.
One. I dropped what I held.
Two. I looked at the blood on my hands.
Three. My vision blurred from tears.
Four. Five. Six.
Nothing.

My mind felt numb. The weight . . . The oppressive, all-consuming weight.

Any thought I had was held hostage by that terrible weight.

The weight of the unforgivable.

I looked over the edge, into that calling abyss.

The price that must be paid.

The burden I couldn't bear.

The sweet embrace of death.

Something else called my name, however.

A voice. The voice. Her voice.

The voice that took my hand and pulled me back from the dark pit of my mind.

I wiped my tears away, smearing blood on my cheeks.

I looked up toward the voice.

The moon was so beautiful that night.

I was so enraptured by it, nearly all other thoughts washed away.

Nearly.

I struggled to remember why I had looked.

I struggled to think of why I should look away.

But . . . that voice. She dragged me back to lucidity.

I tore my eyes away from the silver radiance in the sky.

I looked toward the voice, but my gaze passed over the remains.

The remains of what I had done.

The remains of what little joy and happiness I had in my life.

It all came rushing back like a wave.

The grief that threatened to overwhelm.

Her voice called to me again though, this time more clearly.

I could hear her calling my name.

I had to follow her voice.

I turned my back to it all and followed her voice back into the building.

I walked through those empty halls, following her voice.

It seemed to be only an echo—an echo of a memory.

But it was there. She was here, somewhere.

I heard other things, things I should have questioned,

But her voice made everything else fade away.

The halls were full of that blinding moonlight.

Her voice led me into a room, with a glass wall facing toward the outside.

There was something happening outside, but I couldn't quite see clearly.

The moonlight. The shining, incandescent moonlight. The voice. Her voice.

Before I could give another thought to the commotion outside,

Her voice echoed so clearly in my mind that I could almost feel her breath on my ear.

"Come closer."

I stepped forward, feeling tears well up in my eyes.

I could see something else in the window.

My reflection, approaching nearer.

Something else.

Someone else.

I slowly whispered her name.

"Serena?"

She smiled and beckoned me closer.

I stepped closer and closer to the window.

Something was happening behind her, though, outside of the window.

Things I couldn't quite make out. Things I perhaps didn't want to see.

As though she read my mind, she whispered, "Just look at me. It's all okay now."

She seemed to come into focus not in the reflection, but outside the window itself.

She put her hand up against the glass, repeating, "It's all going to be okay now."

I felt the weight lift from me—that terrible burden I had borne.

Tears blurred my vision as I pressed my hand against hers through the glass.

I could have stayed in that moment for all eternity.

I couldn't tear my gaze away from her eyes.

I couldn't find a voice to speak.

Every word I couldn't say, she seemed to hear.

Every emotion I felt, she seemed to understand.

The fear. The grief. The loss. The pain. The regret. The love.

Her next words resonated in my soul, words that I will never forget.

Words that would change my life forever.

"Matthias, we have work to do."

Matthias took a quick turn and, opening a door, beckoned Joel forward. Joel looked around the lobby—it was entirely empty, with not a person in sight. *I guess they would all be underground, though . . . right?* Joel slowly walked forward and, following Matthias, entered a strange room.

It was very large and filled with rows of chairs, facing toward the outer wall of the building, which was entirely glass, giving a magnificent view of the horizon. The room was uncomfortably bright, lit by many stark white fluorescent lights on the ceiling, the marble floors and walls vaguely reflecting the contents of the room back at Joel. Notably, however, there was no other entrance or exit to the room except for the one behind them.

Joel, realizing this, immediately stopped and turned around, to see the door was now blocked by several members of the group, staring at him blankly. Joel turned back to Matthias, who was smiling at him kindly. Matthias walked to the front of the room and, looking back at Joel, gestured toward one of the chairs.

Joel didn't move an inch, his mind reeling. He stepped back, glancing between Matthias and the guards at the door. Matthias sighed, calmly saying, "Come now, there is nothing to fear. It will be much easier if you simply do as I ask."

Joel opened his mouth to say something, but the words caught in his throat. He frantically glanced around the room, looking for an escape. Matthias frowned and turned away, looking toward the horizon. This immediately prompted several members of the group to march toward Joel.

"Hey, hey—what are you doing? Stop!"

They grabbed Joel by the arms and began moving him. Joel tried to resist, struggling fiercely, but he couldn't throw off the entire group. They dragged him forward, firmly seating him in the chair that Matthias had gestured toward. They then, pulling some strips of fabric out of their bags, tied his arms and legs securely to the arms and legs of the chair.

"What is going on? Stop! Get me out of this—"

Joel stopped his exclamations as Matthias turned back around, smiling at him. Matthias's silvery-gray hair was illuminated brilliantly by the evening sun, and his shadow cast far into the room, covering Joel in darkness.

Matthias gestured toward the guards, prompting them all to exit the room and shut the door behind them. Matthias regarded him for a moment in silence before speaking.

"I'm sure you feel lied to in some way, but I assure you I have been quite honest. I didn't want to have to resort to such uncivilized methods, but you left me no choice. Allow me to explain some—"

Joel cut him off, saying, "Emily knows. She probably ditched her ride and went back to the base; she is going to go find proof in that room of yours and tell everybody."

Matthias smiled, putting his hands behind his back. "As I said, I am quite sure she will be joining us soon. I very much doubt she will tell anybody before she leaves—who else does she trust except for you?"

This has all been a part of the plan. He accounted for every move she made. Joel looked at the ground, quietly saying, "You said you were taking me to the second location. You lied. Does it even exist?"

Matthias frowned, tilting his head. "On the contrary, as I said, I have been . . . quite honest. *This* is the second location. I am going to do nothing to you—despite what you may think, I wish no ill will upon you. I imagine you will be quite happy, even if you don't understand it now. This is for the best, Joel."

His words rang in Joel's head, echoing in his soul. "*This is the second location.*"

Ava and Mom were taken to the second location.

This is the second location.

CHAPTER THIRTEEN

"Matthias, we have work to do."

Emily stepped back from the pulpit, her mind reeling. If Matthias wrote this, then . . . *Joel is in danger.* She turned and sprinted from the room, dashing down the halls. She flew past the two guards, still tied up, as she entered the elevator. Their pleas to be released were silenced as the doors shut behind her.

She stepped back, bracing against the wall of the elevator, feeling faint. *I was right. This whole time I was right. He's . . . He's listening to the sirens too. He's working with them.*

The doors opened to a nearly empty lobby, with only the two guards standing by the doors. She ran between them, their yells echoing behind her. "Hey, it's close to nightfall! Where the hell are you going? You can't stay the night out there!"

As she ran, Emily glanced down at her watch. *7:08 p.m.* She looked up at the sun, which was getting closer to the horizon by the second. She pulled out the map from her back pocket and looked at it—the second location was marked as being a fair distance away, on the very edge of the city. She swore to herself. *I don't have a choice; I have to get down there. I have to take a risk of being outside when the sun sets.*

She quickly made it back to the alley and, to her relief, found the motorcycle was still there. She hopped on and, securing the map in front of the handlebars, started the engine. She quickly exited the alley and, turning toward the horizon, with the sun visible between the rows of buildings, she tore down the road, attempting to stay on the sidewalk to avoid stalled or wrecked cars.

———

Joel felt all thoughts being swept away by tides of emotion. Tears slowly began to flow down his cheeks as he looked at the ground, Matthias's words unheard. He slowly looked up and quietly asked, "Where is Ava?"

Matthias stopped what he had been saying and smiled at Joel. "What do you mean?"

"Where is Ava? I want to see my sister. You said I would see her and Mom. You said they were here."

Matthias tilted his head, seeming confused, before his joyful expression returned. "Ah, I see the confusion. I assure you, I have been entirely honest. I am quite sure you will see your family again. You just have to wait a little bit longer, for the sun to go down."

Despite having asked the question in vain hope and denial, knowing what the answer would be, Joel closed his eyes, grief overwhelming his mind. Matthias frowned, quickly saying, "Please, don't be frightened or saddened. You will be happy this happened once you join them. I truly am doing all this for your own good."

Matthias looked back toward the window, observing the sun. He sighed, pausing for a moment in contemplation, before he said, "I'm afraid I have to leave. I wish I could join you, but I have other work to do for now. Give Emily my regards once she arrives—I'm sure this will be all be easier with her company."

He turned and walked toward the door, leaving Joel sitting in the chair facing the setting sun, eyes still closed, tears running down his cheeks. Joel heard the door firmly close with an echoing boom, leaving him in silence broken only by his own quiet sobbing. He slowly opened his eyes, his vision blurry from tears. It wouldn't be long until nightfall.

———

As Emily flew down the abandoned streets, she tried her best to navigate using the crudely drawn map—it looked as though it was mostly a straight shot to the edge of the city, then just a short drive around the side.

She looked up, squinting her eyes against the blinding light of the sun directly ahead of her. Despite the sky lighting up with deep orange and yellow hues as the day came to an end, it only fueled her panic and determination.

A few minutes passed before her ride was interrupted by another sound, piercing the air above the engine—it was *another* motorcycle engine, getting closer. The sound seemed to overlap itself, getting stronger by the second. *It's the group returning. I need to get the hell off the road before they see me.*

She veered off the sidewalk, down a small feeder road, before turning off the engine momentarily. She pressed herself against the side of a building and turned her head to look toward the road. The noise got louder and louder, until finally motorcycles began passing her, the sound of each increasing to a fever pitch before falling back down to a low rumble in the distance.

All the motorcycles were still laden with bags, and even more worryingly, she counted the number of riders as they passed—each only had one person on it. Joel was missing. She stopped herself from jumping back on her own motorcycle for a few more moments until the group had completely passed and the sounds of the engines had faded into the distance.

She promptly got back on her own motorcycle and, revving the engine, pushed her pace even faster than before. *They can't have just killed him, right? There has to be something else going on here. Please, Joel, hang in there.*

The minutes ticked by, the ambient light getting dimmer and dimmer. She had to be close to the edge of the city but . . . *I'm not going to make it in time.* She felt a rush of fear and panic, both for herself and Joel, before pushing all of it aside to focus entirely on weaving through the streets as fast as possible. *I don't have a choice. I have to get there.*

Joel, trying to clear his head, closed his eyes and breathed deeply. *I need to get out of here. Even if Emily is going to try to get here, there isn't enough time for me to just sit.* He opened his eyes, blinking away the tears again as he tried to judge how much time he had left. The sun had just touched the horizon, bathing the clouds above him in dark orange and red.

He looked down at his restraints—several long strips of cloth tied his arms and legs to the chair. *It isn't rope, so maybe it isn't as strong.* He began yanking his arms up as hard as he could, trying to loosen the restraints enough to let him slip out of them. They didn't give, though—both the chair and the fabric held their form, not releasing Joel from his prison.

Joel yelled in frustration, the anger that had been fueling him slowly fading as he exhausted himself. Panic crept in to replace the anger, however, as the sun dipped farther below the horizon. Hysteria began taking over, his controlled efforts turning into wild movements as he attempted to free himself.

The outdoors became darker and darker until, finally, the last drops of sunlight faded below the horizon. Joel stopped, breathing heavily, his eyes scanning the outdoors.

Several moments passed in silence before the lights above him flickered once and burned out, leaving Joel in absolute darkness. Without any other lights, he could see a vague outline of his own reflection in the glass in front of him.

A different light began overtaking the sky—a dim glow manifested from a point in the sky above him, from an origin

Joel couldn't see. He assumed it was moonlight, but the light began increasing in strength before his eyes, quickly expanding and filling the room he was in with the same oppressive silver light that overtook the outdoors. He felt his strength and energy fading, as if the light itself was draining him.

Joel jumped and screamed as the sirens began, their shrieks piercing into his mind, unblocked by anything but the sleek glass wall in front of him. He couldn't have moved even if he wasn't restrained—the sirens bored into his soul, leaving him completely vulnerable.

There was nothing through the window that he could see—no creatures, no anomalies, just the excruciatingly bright moonlight, covering every surface of the outdoors. The light somehow seemed to get even brighter, almost blinding his vision. He could clearly see his reflection in the glass now, despite the details being lost due to the moderate distance between him and the wall.

Joel began to weep, unable to do anything to fight against the sirens as they clawed their way in. Strangely, however, soon after the noise began, it began fading, into the dull, hazy background of his awareness. Joel gasped in relief, shaking his head and closing his eyes—but just as soon as he did, he felt a force trying to pull his gaze back outside. He fought the urge for a moment before he slowly opened his eyes again and looked back toward the outdoors.

"Hey, Joel."

Joel flinched slightly at Kayla's voice, though he didn't look away from the moonlight. He slowly responded, "Kayla? Is that you?"

"Of course it's me, who else would it be?" He almost envisioned her smiling at him as she said this.

"Why are you here? Did you know Matthias was going to do this to me?"

Again, he could almost see her as she sighed, and her expression shifted into a small frown.

"This would have happened anyway—I think you know that. It was only a matter of time."

The moonlight seemed to soften a bit—slowly changing from feeling invasive and painful to look at to being . . . almost inviting. There was a small pause before Kayla softly said, "This is for the best, Joel."

"But . . . I don't want to go. I . . . Ava needs me . . . She could still be here somewhere, maybe Mom got her out before . . . before . . ." Joel felt tears well up in his eyes, not even believing his own words. Something caught his eye outside—he looked at it, breaking his transfixion. A chill ran down his spine as he realized it was in the *reflection,* not outside.

It looked like a figure was sitting in the chair next to him. He quickly looked, his panic overtaking his mind for a moment—but, the chair was empty. As his panic faded, his head quickly snapped back to the window.

"I really am sorry—I don't want this to be hard for you. I hope you know that."

Joel slowly nodded, tears running down his cheeks. The figure in the reflection became clearer as he listened—he could distinctly see long, curly black hair. After a few more moments, he could see Kayla in the reflection, with a sad smile on her face as she looked at him.

"I . . . I know, Kayla. I believe you."

Kayla smiled in the reflection and reached her hand out to lay it on his arm. He didn't feel anything, though, again causing his mesmerized state to break as he looked down at his arm, to see nothing there. He looked back up at the reflection—Kayla was gone.

Joel scanned the window frantically, wanting to see her again. The moonlight seemed to get brighter for a moment, causing his gaze to return back to the sky. A few moments passed before Kayla's voice returned.

"Stay focused—I want to be here for you, but I can't if you don't let me in. Do you want me to stay?"

Joel nodded, relief washing over him as Kayla's visage slowly appeared in the reflection again. She smiled at him, her hand squeezing his arm gently—this time, he did feel her gentle, caring touch. "Good. There is someone else who wants to see you, but you have to let her in too—you have to accept what happened for you to see her. Do you want to see her?"

Joel slowly nodded, tears running down his cheeks.

———

Emily pushed at a breakneck pace, panic starting to overtake her mind again as she saw more and more of the sun disappear behind the horizon, the light fading around her every second. Finally, she saw a break in the high-rises—the edge of the city.

She looked down at her map—judging from the road that she thought she was on, the second location should be just six buildings down to her left after she got to the perimeter.

Suddenly, she felt something wrong deep inside her. She

slowed dramatically, swerving, as her stomach twisted into knots. She came to a halt, breathing heavily.

She glanced up—the sun had disappeared below the horizon. She almost looked up at the sky, but she quickly stopped herself, freezing in place. She didn't even want to look, but something deep inside her was attempting to twist her gaze to the sky.

Her adrenaline spiked, recalling what happened to Jeremy after he succeeded in going outside. *He turned himself over to look at something in the sky. This is the end game of the sirens—they want you to look up at . . . something.*

Her head twitched as she fought for control. She shook her head, a cold determination overtaking her. *Do not look up. Just get there. Do not look up.*

She quickly reached into her pockets and pushed in her earplugs, just in time for a sudden wall of sound to hit her. She almost fell over, stumbling and catching herself before she tipped the bike. She closed her eyes, gritting her teeth as her ears radiated with excruciating pain.

She took several quick breaths, opening her eyes and seating herself back on the bike, then revved the engine. The city was awash with a silvery glow from above, and frighteningly, it seemed to be getting brighter by the moment. She felt her head twitch upward again, causing a rush of panic to pass through her as she jerked it back down, keeping her eyes fixed on the road in front of her.

Don't look up, don't look up, don't look up ... She repeated the phrase in her head as she drove, keeping her focus away from the otherworldly screeches of the sirens and the impulse to look toward the sky. She breathed heavily, finally approaching the edge of the city. She could feel her will waning—she could feel the sirens breaking in, wriggling and writhing in her mind.

She slowly let her gaze wander up as she counted the buildings—*one, two, three, four, five* ... As she got to the sixth building, her gaze drifted upward just a bit farther against her will, past the top of the building. Her eyes widened, and she felt an overwhelming sense of dread overtake her.

She snapped her head down, the image of the moon, incandescent with silver light, burning into her mind. *It's just the moon. There's nothing up there, just the moon.* She wanted to look again, though ... She shook her head, her panic rising. *I looked.* She felt a sudden calm overtake her as her eyes drifted upward against her will, her mind screaming in protest.

She stopped herself, adrenaline again bursting through her as her eyes landed on a figure in the building in front of her, tied down to a chair in front of a glass wall. *Joel.* All her other thoughts washed away as she took control of her body again, quickly dismounting the vehicle and sprinting toward the front door.

She stumbled to the side for a moment, her head pounding and her mind in a daze. The visage of the moon was burned into her vision—she could still see it, though it was a faint memory of the firsthand view she'd experienced. Again, her head twitched upward as she fought for control. She crossed the rest of the distance in a stupor, crashing through the doors of the building.

———

Kayla smiled, nodding. Joel closed his eyes, feeling a calm embrace him. When he opened them again, he saw another shadowy form, sitting in the chair to his other side.

BOOM.

Joel jumped, snapping back to reality as his head whipped around to see Emily crashing through the door, causing it to slam against the wall. Kayla's touch disappeared from his arm as Joel turned his attention to Emily, the daze of the sirens quickly replaced with confusion and elation at the sight of her.

She looked almost frenzied, as though she wasn't completely in control of her actions. She stumbled forward, reaching into her back pocket and pulling out her engraved pocketknife.

"Oh my god, Emily, are you OK? You were . . . out there."

Emily didn't respond, dropping to her knees in front of him as she flipped the blade of the knife open. She quickly severed the restraints on his legs, then his arms, before attempting to stand back up. She keeled to the side, however, falling into the chairs. Joel sprang up and, grabbing her beneath the arms, pulled her back from the window to the rear of the room.

"Emily, are you still with me? Come on, we've got to get out of here."

Emily mumbled something, her eyes opening to look past Joel, through the window. Joel attempted to go through the door, but Emily suddenly jerked, pulling against his restraint.

"Emily? Emily, what's wrong, talk to me!"

"Matthias—he . . . You . . . I can't think. I . . . I need to go, Joel. I need to see it again!"

Emily's voice rose as she talked, her gaze still fixed toward the window. Joel struggled to hold her as she wiggled back and forth in his grasp.

"What do you mean? Emily, we're OK now, we just need to find someplace to hide for the night, as far inside as we can—" Joel turned her head, forcibly breaking her eye contact with the light. She suddenly stopped fighting, gasping for breath.

Emily swayed, holding her head in her hands. Joel grabbed her by the shoulders, asking, "What's going on? What happened out there?"

Tears began streaming down Emily's cheeks—her eyes were wide, staring into nothing. She opened her mouth as if to say something, but then her gaze darted back to the glass. Joel quickly grabbed on to her tightly as she began fighting again, screaming, "It has me! Joel, it has me—I can't get it out of my head! I can't fight it!"

Joel, shifting his weight, swung Emily around so she was facing the back wall. Emily snapped out of it again as her gaze broke from the outdoors, her posture relaxing momentarily as she reached out to grab on to Joel. She whispered, "I can't fight it, Joel. It's too late."

"Emily, look at me—you are going to be OK, you aren't going to give in. We are going to make it through this. We just need to get away from the walls, get inside—"

Joel's sentence broke off as Emily's head jerked back toward the outdoors. She slipped free from his grasp for a moment, stumbling forward toward the light. Joel leapt forward to grab her, causing them both to fall to the ground. Joel tried to hold her down, but she writhed wildly.

"Emily! Focus, look at me, don't look outside."

Emily began crying, struggling even more than before. Her eyes were wide and bloodshot, unblinking, staring outside. She seemed to break free for a moment, her gaze prying away with the light for a heartbeat before returning. "Please, Joel, I can't . . . Don't let me go out there. Don't let them take me!" She then immediately screamed, "No! Let me go! Please, I need to go! This is what I'm supposed to do!"

The wailing of the sirens returned to Joel's awareness, causing him to feel faint for a moment as he felt them struggle to get back in. He gritted his teeth and, ignoring the mental assault, yelled over the noise, "What do you mean? Emily, what happened out there?"

Emily's gaze broke from the glass again, panic flashing in her eyes. "The sirens! The sirens, Joel! Don't let them use my voice—don't let them use me to get into your head! The gun!"

A flurry of thoughts ran through Joel's mind as he quickly became aware of the gun hidden in Emily's waistband. Suddenly, he realized what she was asking him to do. He opened his mouth to respond, but no sound came out.

Emily arched her spine, her eyes rolling back into her head for a moment before she stopped again, weakly saying, "Please, I can't . . ." Her voice broke, turning into a shriek.

"I can see it, it's in my mind! I can't resist—it compels me!" She grimaced and, closing her eyes, shook her head again, breathlessly whispering, "I can't keep control—please, Joel, you have to do it! Don't let me go out there! Don't let me . . . don't let me join them . . . please . . ."

Her voice drifted off before she resumed her fight to break free of Joel's grasp, screaming, "Let me go! Please, Joel, let me go! I need to go!" Joel didn't know what to do—he felt his muscles weakening, and he felt his mind giving in to the unrelenting tirade of the sirens again. He was frozen, unable to say or do anything but hold her down.

The sirens drilled into his mind, their assault different this time than any of the previous nights. They weren't trying to get him to listen—they were trying to subdue him. Joel felt his strength fading.

Finally, his hold on her broke. As she began crawling away, Joel lunged forward and snatched the gun from her waistband. He glanced between it and Emily, who tried to scramble to her feet before suddenly lurching to the side, crashing into the wall next to the door, as she shrieked, "Please!"

Joel, tears running down his cheeks, used his last ounce of strength before the sirens incapacitated him to raise the gun and pull the trigger.

CHAPTER FOURTEEN

Joel's ears rang as the gun fell from his hand. He collapsed to the side, closing his eyes as his head hit the floor with a thud. He felt paralyzed, unable to move or think. The sirens' cries momentarily faded as they were pushed out of his mind, grief and shock flooding in to take their place.

He felt as though he couldn't breathe—waves of emotion began rolling through him, each one more intense than the last. Anger, denial, and guilt pressed in on him from all sides, constricting his thoughts. Suddenly, however, a chill ran up his spine as he felt something else enter his mind.

"Joel . . ."

Kayla's voice was soft and sympathetic. Joel kept his eyes closed, not moving, tears slowly running down his cheeks and pooling onto the floor. He welcomed her into his mind, the weight of his grief lessening as she pushed it out of the way.

"You didn't have to do that, Joel. She would have been waiting for you, like I am."

He felt her hand on his shoulder—a comforting warmth spread across his body as he embraced her presence, clinging to any shred of happiness to keep himself from falling back into the swirling abyss of his emotions. He breathed deeply, regaining control of his body. A few moments passed in silence before Kayla's voice cut through his mind again.

"You don't have to go back there, if you don't want to. You can leave all of it behind, you just have to come with me."

Joel slowly shook his head, whispering, "I can't. You know I can't."

He could almost feel Kayla's emotions—he could sense the slightest disappointment at his words before empathy flooded her mind. He could feel her squeeze his shoulder as she responded, "You can now. You have nothing left here— you have no reason to stay."

He felt more and more of his mind giving way to her. She was right—everything he had been fighting for, everything he had been *surviving* for, was gone. He slowly nodded, feeling the weight of all his emotions slowly lifting. *This is for the best.* As the thought passed through him, a memory from earlier that day flashed through his mind. Matthias, standing in front of him with his hands behind his back, firmly saying, *"This is for the best, Joel."*

Joel's eyes snapped open as anger and panic flooded through him. He retaliated against the foreign presence in his mind, letting his anger push it out. He turned and swung out his arm where he felt Kayla, but hit nothing but air. He sat up and crawled back against the wall, facing the glass wall, the unnatural moonlight flooding the room.

As he looked up, he saw Emily's lifeless body lying limp on the ground. His throat tightened and nausea flooded through him as he closed his eyes again, shock paralyzing his mind. *What have I done?* The moment his guard lowered, the sirens pushed back into his awareness.

"Look at me, Joel."

Joel's eyes instinctively opened at the command. His vision was blurry, but after several blinks he saw Kayla through the glass, outside the building. She was standing with her hands clasped in front of her, her hair falling loosely around her shoulders, looking down at him with a sad expression.

Joel slowly stood, his gaze fixed on her. The light seemed to get softer as Joel relaxed again, shrouding the outdoors in a comforting silver glow. He trudged toward the glass, unable to move his gaze. Halfway across the room, however, his trance was broken as he kicked something, causing it to skid across the floor.

His eyes fell, following the gun as it approached and hit the glass with a sharp clink. He quickly looked away and stepped back from the glass as he regained control of his actions. *Stop! Don't let them get into your head. Emily . . . she died saving you. Don't let it be in vain.* He marched away from the wall, the light increasing in intensity for a moment before returning to how it was. He shook his head, breathing heavily, before exiting the room.

The lobby of the building was heavily exposed to the outdoors, the majority of the outer walls glass in keeping with the modern design. He turned, walking farther into the building. There were several rooms similar to the one he had just been in, and a long hallway near the far edge of the building. Steeling himself, he slowly walked to the hallway.

The entire hallway was glowing with moonlight, the glass outer wall providing no protection, much like the rest of the building. He slowly began trudging down it, looking for a room to hide in. His search was soon interrupted, however.

"Please, Joel, I am trying to help you."

Joel's head twitched toward the glass, but he stopped himself. Breathing slowly, he ignored Kayla's voice as he walked farther down the hall. There was a prolonged silence, broken only by his echoing footsteps. *Why can I still hear her? Why am I not hearing the sirens like usual? I'm fighting, so why is it still like I'm under their spell?*

"Because you aren't fighting. There's still a part of you that is letting me in—and I think you know that too. Because . . . you know who else is with me."

Joel closed his eyes and, gritting his teeth, kept moving. He felt sadness and empathy radiating from Kayla, which again caused him to question himself. *Why can I still feel her?* Kayla's response came quickly, whispering into his soul.

"Because you know I'm real. And that makes you want to look to see if Ava is real too."

Anger flared in Joel's mind, and, his eyes snapping open, he turned to face the glass. Kayla was in the reflection, walking beside him. He yelled and slammed his hand against the glass. "Stop! You don't even know her! You don't know her name—I never told you her name! How do you know her name?"

Joel slid onto his knees as tears began to flow down his cheeks. In the reflection, Kayla slowly walked behind him and, pursing her lips, seemed to walk into the glass. She disappeared as she passed to the other side, leaving Joel kneeling, his face in his hands, alone.

Several moments passed before a timid voice broke the silence.

"Joel?"

Joel's head slowly lifted. He looked outside to see a small girl standing on the other side of the glass. Joel's eyes widened and everything else around him faded away. "Ava?"

Ava's hair was glowing softly in the moonlight and she was wearing the same fuzzy hoodie that she had on when Joel last saw her. Her eyes were wide, and she seemed unsure, if not frightened.

She slowly stepped forward and put her hands up against the glass. Joel reached one of his hands up and pressed it against hers through the glass. Ava's bottom lip trembled slightly as she whispered, "I'm scared. I wish you had gone with us."

Joel felt tears welling up in his eyes as he struggled to respond. "Ava, I wish I had gone with you too. I can't tell you how much I wish I had. But I can't now. It's . . . It's . . ." *But it's too late.*

Ava nodded but, after a few moments, her bottom lip trembled again, and tears began flowing down her cheeks. She wiped her eyes with the cuffs of her hoodie and, taking shaky, quick breaths, looked as though she was trying to hide her crying.

Joel closed his eyes, putting his forehead on the cold glass. *I can't do this.* "Please, I . . . I can't. I know you aren't . . . I know you aren't . . ." Joel began sobbing, his throat tightening and his chest heaving as he struggled to breathe.

Ava's next whisper was so quiet he could barely hear it, but it cut through his soul. "I can't get in. Joey, please, I can't get in. You have to come get me."

Joel opened his eyes and looked up. Ava was pushing her tiny hands tightly against the glass. She was sniffling, holding back tears. She meekly hit the glass with both of her fists before sitting on the ground and, putting her face in her hands, softly crying.

It's not her . . . It's not her . . . Just keep moving. Joel, taking a deep, shaky breath, slowly said, "OK . . . Ava, listen to me. Just walk around the side of the building, to the doors. I'll come get you, OK?"

Ava looked up, her eyes red and puffy. She slowly nodded, her chin trembling. She pushed herself up and, pointing off to the side, quietly asked, "That way?"

"Yes, just put your hand on the wall and walk until you find the doors. I'll be waiting right there for you, don't be scared."

Ava slowly nodded and, looking frightened, put her hand against the glass and started to cautiously walk. Joel closed his eyes, taking several deep breaths. *I'm so sorry, Ava.*

Joel stood and, once Ava disappeared around the corner

of the building, pushed all his thoughts and instincts down as he jerkily began walking in the opposite direction, toward the other end of the hall. He barely made it a few steps in that direction before a different voice broke the air.

"What are you doing?"

His mom's voice startled Joel, but he kept his eyes fixed ahead of him. Gritting his teeth, he stopped himself from replying. He saw something moving alongside him in his peripheral vision, keeping pace in the reflection.

"Do you even care about Ava? Maybe it's for the best that she is here with me."

Joel's nostrils flared as he felt anger welling. He kept trudging forward, slowly approaching the end of the hall. *Don't take the bait, just keep walking.*

"I mean honestly, if you cared about either of us, you would have come into the city on that first night to find us. But I don't even know why I expected that of you."

Joel closed his eyes, coming to an abrupt halt in the hallway. He breathed in slowly, trying to keep his mind clear. *She told me not to try to go into the city. It was safest for all of us.*

"That's typical, not even going to respond to me. Why do I even try?"

Joel slowly shook his head, simply saying, "You aren't Mom. You haven't been for a long time."

He abruptly continued walking and, as he exited the hallway into a stairwell, he heard her call after him, her voice shaking slightly, "What do you mean? Joel, wait!"

Her pleading voice dug into Joel's mind, but he attempted to ignore the impulse to look back as he approached the stairs; there were windows lining every floor. *That figures.* He slowly climbed the stairs, fatigue wearing him down.

Joel was careful not to look outside as he ascended and, after reaching the next floor, threw the door open to reveal an identical hallway as the one below him. Swearing under his breath, he started walking down the hall. Almost immediately, he saw his mom join him in the reflection.

"Joel, please, I . . . You know I care about you, right? You're still my son, no matter . . . no matter what happened. I'm . . . I'm sorry I was harsh; I shouldn't have said those things back there. I just want you to be with us. And now that you're here, and we're telling you that you can be . . . why . . . why aren't you trying to? Do you even *want* to be with us?"

Joel stammered before hesitantly replying, "W-what do you mean? I've been looking for you two this entire time! The only reason I came into the city was to find you."

His mom's hand reached forward toward him, but she stopped herself as a sad expression came over her face.

She quietly responded, "You didn't come into the city to find *us*, Joel. You came into the city to find Ava."

Joel stopped walking and, closing his eyes, felt a cold wave of guilt wash over him. He opened his mouth to respond, but no words came out. He shook his head and meekly choked out, "No, I . . . That's not true. Mom, you know that's not true. You can't just . . . You can't . . ."

Joel stopped mid-sentence, feeling a lump forming in the back of his throat. He took a deep breath and tried to push down the emotions attempting to take control of him. *They aren't real, Joel. They aren't real. Fight back, damn you.* Joel fell to his knees as he wrestled for control, doubling over. He reached up and, gripping the back of his head so tightly that he could feel hair ripping from his scalp, screamed, "Get out! Get out of my head! Stop manipulating me—stop using them against me!"

When he looked up again, his mom and Ava were gone. He was alone in the reflection, and in the hallway. He released his grip on his head and his chest convulsed momentarily as he let out a small sob. He shook his head and, after catching his breath and steeling himself, pushed himself up off the ground and continued walking through the hall into the lobby of the second floor.

It looked like an exact replica of the floor below him, with the exception of the front doors being replaced with another smooth glass wall. *What the hell kind of building is this?* As he shuffled forward, he saw a figure standing outside where the front doors should have been. It was Ava, her hands beating meekly on the glass.

You lied to her. You abandoned her. What kind of brother are you? Joel turned and, fighting away tears, yelled, "Get out of my head! Stop!" He braced against a sleek metallic wall as he struggled to regain control of his thoughts.

"I think you know that isn't us. We can't control your own thoughts and feelings."

He saw Kayla standing behind him in the dim, gray reflection of the wall, a sad expression on her face. Joel shook his head, saying, "B-but I didn't abandon her, or lie to her. I know that isn't her out there. You can't tell me that's actually her!"

He firmly pointed to the front door before noticing there was now nothing outside the glass but the city, radiant with silver light. He bit his lip and, shaking his head, turned back to the wall. Kayla was standing behind him again, not saying anything. She slowly approached and, setting her hand on his shoulder, quietly said, "I *am* telling you that that's actually her. She just wants to be with you again. She loves you and relies on you."

Joel's throat tightened as Kayla spoke. His chin trembled

for a moment before he weakly replied, "But . . . that would mean that I did lie to her. That would mean . . ." His statement drifted off as he closed his eyes, putting his head against the wall.

"It's OK, she—and we all—understand. This is . . . a lot to take in. We just want you to be—"

Joel interrupted her, yelling, "Stop messing with my emotions!" He turned and walked away, toward the closest room. He threw the door open and entered, to see an identical room to the one downstairs, with chairs lining almost the entire width of the room, facing out to the glass wall. He immediately turned to leave, but Kayla's voice stopped him.

"Wait! I want to show you something, please. Give me a chance."

He resisted for a moment, standing frozen in the doorway, before he turned around to face back toward Kayla. She was standing outside the glass, smiling at him. She beckoned him forward, nodding encouragingly.

Joel slowly walked to the glass, unable to look away. Once he got close, Kayla said, "Good. I want you to sit down in that chair in the front, OK? I'll sit right next to you, and I want you to watch the reflection closely."

Joel didn't move, staring into Kayla's eyes. *It's not just like*

I'm seeing a vision of Kayla, I'm just . . . seeing Kayla. He quietly whispered, "How can I trust you?"

Kayla tilted her head, seeming hurt for a moment. "What do you mean?"

Joel shook his head, thinking, before slowly saying, "I can't just . . . How can I trust what you, or any of you, are telling me, if I don't know that you're . . . ?" His question drifted off as he struggled to put into words what he was asking.

Kayla nodded in understanding before quietly asking, "Well . . . Do you think I'm . . . me?"

"I . . . I don't know anymore."

Kayla nodded before she quietly said, "Do you want to see what I have to show you, then? Please, I really think this will help you."

Joel slowly nodded, his internal struggle against the compulsion quickly fading as he walked over and sat down, carefully watching the reflection in the glass. Just as Kayla said, soon after he sat down Kayla appeared to walk in from the side of the room and quickly sat down in the chair to his right, smiling. "Perfect. We are going to do this just like we did before, OK? Just relax."

He felt peace wash over him as she talked, making him slowly relax, both physically and mentally. Kayla nodded encouragingly, squeezing his arm gently. "Now, just look into the reflection. For this to work, I really need you to believe this is real, OK?"

He slowly nodded, unable to tear his gaze from the reflection. A few moments passed before a small figure walked in and sat herself in the chair next to him. Ava beamed up at him and, without hesitation, she leaned sideways and wrapped her arms around him, laying her head on his arm. Joel felt all his fears and doubts lift from him, the entirety of his being focused solely on Ava's embrace.

"A-Ava, I'm so sorry. I didn't want . . . I didn't want . . ."

"It's OK. I'm glad you're here now."

Joel started to look down at her, but Kayla quietly whispered, "Keep looking at the reflection, don't look away. It won't be real anymore if you look away. I'm just trying to show you what it will be like."

Joel was unable to respond for a moment, but quietly choked out, "Like what will be like?"

The next response startled him for an instant, as it was his mom's voice, not Kayla's.

"What it will be like when you join us. We . . . We can try again, Joel. I know things were hard for a while there, but . . ."

Joel's throat tightened and he felt a cold anger fall over

him. "You *know* things were hard? You were the *reason* things were hard! After Dad left, you just . . . you shut down. You left me . . . You left us." Joel's voice wavered as he struggled to control the emotions washing over him.

His mom looked sadly at him and, after a moment, a tear ran down her face. She nodded and said, "I know. Joel, I'm so sorry for doing that to you. I'm sorry that I put so much responsibility on you to care for Ava . . . and me. I can't ask for you to forgive that, but . . . I want to try again. I want to try to make us a real family again, and leave all that behind."

Joel's anger slowly faded and was replaced by a deep sorrow. Tears ran down his cheeks as he struggled to respond. Ava tightly hugged his arm and, mumbling into it, softly said, "Please, Joey? Please. I want to be able to sit with you and hug you for real again. I want to tell you about that movie you missed."

Joel shut his eyes and let a small sob escape. Before he could respond, his mom chimed in. "Your sister needs you, Joel. I need you. You know what you need to do."

Joel concentrated as hard as he could on his thoughts. He let everything else fade away, leaving him alone. For a brief moment, he felt as though a hold on his mind was released—a pressure that he wasn't sure how long he had been pushing back against. *I can't forget, but I do forgive you, Mom. I'm sorry I didn't try to reconnect with you, or appreciate the moments we did share. I hope you can forgive me now for this.*

Fighting against every desire in his being, he abruptly stood, ignoring the voices and visages of his mom and Ava. He turned and, with monumental effort in each step, walked away from the window and out of the room. He felt faint for a moment, his vision fading in and out, forcing him to stumble and catch himself against the wall. As he caught his breath, a voice interrupted him.

"Why can't you let go? There's no reason to stay. You'd be much happier if you came with us, I promise."

Joel looked up at Kayla, who was giving him a confused look, her head tilted. Joel shook his head, replying, "There is a reason. I can't let Emily to have died for nothing. This is more important than whether or not I want to be with my family, or even whether or not I believe you."

Kayla opened her mouth to respond, but she gave him a sad look and nodded. She slowly approached and, gently putting her hand on his shoulder, said, "I understand, I really do. I think I might know how to make this easier for you."

Joel looked up and, meeting her eyes, raised an eyebrow. "What do you mean?"

"If you can't come with us until you find peace here, then

that's OK. If you don't want us to bother you, that's OK too. We can wait—but you have to really promise me that you'll do what you need to do tomorrow, and that you'll be ready to talk again tomorrow night. OK?"

Joel blinked, unsure of what to make of her response. "You'll wait, as in . . . ?"

Kayla nodded, smiling sadly. "Yup, as in you won't hear a peep for the rest of the night. You can rest and think without any of us bothering you."

Joel rubbed his forehead, thinking. *She's right. If I can deal with Matthias and finish what Emily started, I won't have any reason to stay. And . . . I do want to be with Ava . . . and Mom.* Joel slowly nodded, saying, "All right. I'll . . . I'll see you tomorrow night, then."

Kayla smiled and, turning around, quietly said, "Good luck, Joel. I really do hope you can find peace tomorrow. I just want you to be happy—all of us do."

Joel closed his eyes for a moment as he felt a pressure release from his mind. He opened his eyes to find he was entirely alone, in utter silence. The moonlight outside was normal, bathing the outdoors in dim, gray light, and shining in through the windows enough to allow Joel to see.

As his thoughts cleared, he felt a tide of emotions flow in that had been held back, restricted from entering his mind while the sirens were present. *Emily, I'm so sorry.* He turned and slowly slid down the wall, feeling waves of nausea roll through his body. His throat constricted and he felt a numbness fall over his entire body.

He wrapped his arms around his chest, gripping his shirt tightly, as his body convulsed with wracking sobs. He lay down, back toward the empty room, and pressed his forehead against the cold wall as he let his grief flow through him.

What have I done?

CHAPTER FIFTEEN

Joel's dreams were chaotic, despite not being under the influence of the sirens—he saw intermittent flashes of people, each mouthing unheard words to him. He was caught in the swirling abyss of his emotions, submerged in waves of guilt, anger, and despair. He could hardly stay asleep as he kept jerking awake in a cold sweat, before falling back into a feverish, fretful state of unconsciousness.

Joel's eyes snapped open again as he pulled himself from the nightmares, gasping. It was still nighttime, the room dimly lit by the gray moonlight flowing in from the windows—though, the horizon to the east was very faintly glowing red. He crawled away from the wall, trying to clear his head.

He slowly pushed himself off the ground, arms shaking profusely—he wasn't sure if it was from the freezing cold or the lingering trauma of his dreams. He was still completely alone and in utter silence—Kayla seemed to have kept her word.

The horizon to the east, though still mostly enveloped in darkness, had a steadily growing sliver of light, with the first gleanings of color returning to the sky. He slowly shambled to the window, grimacing as a splitting headache began forming.

He stood in silence in front of the window, waiting to watch the sunrise, his mind blank and numb. Hunger and thirst clawed at him, but that was the last thing he was concerned about right now. He gritted his teeth, pushing down his quickly welling emotions. *Where do I even go from here?*

A small circlet of deep red and orange began creeping up from the horizon, headed by the first touches of blue. Joel sighed, rubbing his head and closing his eyes as he thought about the events from last night and his conversation with Kayla. *"I really do hope you can find peace tomorrow."*

He opened his eyes again, squinting against the quickly growing light. *There's only one route forward, but I don't even know what will come of it. If I want to honor Emily's death, I need to go try to stop Matthias. I can't let her death mean nothing.*

His own words from last night rang in his head. *It's more important than whether or not I believe you—what does that even mean? If I'm willing to consider that they are real, and that in some way they are actually wanting the best for me . . . then what does that mean about Emily?*

Joel closed his eyes for a moment, exhaling slowly, before pushing the thoughts out of his head to observe the sunrise. The first edge of the sun had just peeked over the horizon, bathing the clouds above him in a light pink and bathing the sky in light blue, but leaving the city in darkness.

No matter what, I need to at least go try to confront Matthias. Despite the sun being clearly visible in the sky now, he was still apprehensive about going outside. Normally, he would know when the sirens stopped in the morning—but now, without their presence, he wasn't entirely sure when it was safe. *No time like the present.*

He turned from the window and began slowly walking down the length of the building to the stairwell. His footsteps echoed in the empty halls, cutting through the silence. He shielded his eyes from the reflections of the sun in the glass until he reached the end of the hallway and, pulling the door open, entered into the stairwell.

Joel winced as his stiff muscles sent dull waves of pain up his legs every time he descended a step. Alongside his growing hunger and thirst, his body was teetering on the edge of failure. *I'm so tired.* The windows on each floor provided more than enough light for Joel to slowly make his way down the steps before exiting onto the first floor, relieved that he could walk on level ground.

As he passed through the hallway, he could almost hear his mom's words from last night—he could almost see Ava, standing outside the glass, trying to hide her tears. *Was Kayla right? If that was actually Ava . . .* Joel gritted his teeth and, reaching the end of the hall, turned to face the lobby. All the doors were shut, but Joel's eyes immediately wandered to the one that Emily had crashed through the night before to save him. He stopped as he passed it, closing his eyes.

A part of him wanted to check, but he didn't even know what he would be checking for—he knew what he would see. After a long moment, Joel slowly shook his head and continued walking, a lump forming in his throat. *I'm sorry, Emily.*

He approached the front doors of the building and, after gathering himself, cautiously pushed them open. He tensed for a moment, almost expecting something horrible to happen as he entered the outdoors, but all he got was a gentle, chilly breeze and fresh air. There was a motorcycle parked right in front of the building, with a piece of paper pinned to the handlebars.

Joel approached it, realizing with a sinking heart that it was the one Emily had used to get here. The keys were still in the ignition, but the engine was off. He looked down at the crudely drawn map and attempted to orient himself based on the labeled buildings.

If I drive down a few buildings to the right, then it's almost a straight shot directly back to base. Joel slowly lifted himself onto the seat of the vehicle and, turning the key and pushing down the ignition switch, started the engine. He looked toward the building one more time, a cascade of emotions flowing through him, before he turned the bike and, slowly accelerating, began driving away.

He stopped himself from looking back again, blinking tears out of his eyes. Emily's words to him from several days ago came crashing back into his consciousness. *"Right, focus on the* now. *Keep moving."* Joel slowly exhaled, focusing on the road ahead of him.

He drove mostly on the sidewalks to steer clear of the wreckage—though many days had passed since this first began, the city had been left unrecognizable. Normally these streets would be bustling with morning activity, people walking along the sidewalks, each with their own life—but now, he was the only thing disturbing the silence.

Joel looked up at the sun, trying to gauge the time. *I don't know exactly how long I've been riding, but . . . the base has to be close. I'd better get off the road with this thing, so I don't get spotted.* Joel pulled his ride off the sidewalk into an alley and, parking it, slowly slid off. He looked down at the map, trying to judge where he could be.

Since I didn't make any turns, it should be somewhere to my left up ahead, down a different road. I guess I just need to walk and look. Making a mental note of where the motorcycle was, he folded the map and put it in his back pocket as he slowly exited the alley and began walking down the road.

A few minutes later, his progress was interrupted by a call to his right. "Hey! Who're you?"

Joel slowly looked right, unperturbed. There were three people on the other side of the road, all of whom were carrying large bags of something. As Joel looked over, their eyes widened. Joel closed his eyes for a moment and sighed, too numb to feel anything as he recognized them too. All three of them were a part of Matthias's crew that took him and Emily out to the second location.

They all dropped their bags and, quickly crossing the street, approached Joel. "How the hell did you . . . ?" As they asked the question, Joel raised a hand, quietly saying, "I need to talk to Matthias. Take me to him."

They looked at one another, unsure of what to do. Joel stared at them blankly, waiting for a response. Finally, one of them said, "Yeah, we were going to take you back to him anyway. He will want to talk to you. Follow us, don't try anything stupid."

The one who spoke turned and began walking. The other two stepped behind Joel and, giving him a firm push, prodded him forward. Joel wordlessly followed the leader, falling in line behind him. *What am I even going to do? How am I supposed to . . . resolve this?* Joel shook his head, letting his mind clear, as he fell back into a stupor of numbing apathy, letting the minutes pass in silence.

"All right, we're almost here. Don't talk to anyone until we get to Matthias's office, you understand? One toe out of line and you are out." Joel looked up, half aware of the words, nodding slowly. The leader stared at him for a moment before turning and continuing toward the building at the end of the road ahead of them.

A minute later, they entered the front lobby of the building. It was packed with people, organized into groups, about to go out on their missions for the day. Several people looked at Joel and his escorts curiously but didn't say anything. After a short elevator ride, they emerged at the top floor. One of the men held Joel back, saying, "Wait here while we tell Matthias what's going on."

Joel didn't respond, staring past them all and looking outside through the window ahead of him. One guard stayed with Joel, but the other two disappeared down the hall to the right. Several moments later, quick footsteps came back down the hall.

"Joel?"

Joel glanced toward the voice, everything else fading away as he made eye contact with Matthias. He looked bewildered, both eyebrows raised and his head tilted. Joel didn't respond as he struggled to control his emotions. Matthias's composure returned after a moment as he said, "Please, come with me."

Joel didn't move, paralyzed by emotions and indecision, staring intensely at Matthias. After a moment, Matthias frowned at him and gestured toward the guards, saying, "Bring him into my office."

The guards grabbed both of Joel's arms and, firmly pulling him forward, led him down the hall. As they arrived at Matthias's office, they pushed Joel into the room, releasing him. Matthias quickly said, "Easy, don't throw him around. Please, shut the door and let us talk for a few moments in peace."

Joel looked back at the guards who, after a moment of hesitation, did as Matthias asked, firmly closing the door behind Joel. He turned back to look at Matthias, who was regarding him thoughtfully. Matthias gestured toward the chair in front of his desk, saying, "Please, sit. I believe we have some things to talk about."

Despite his best effort, as Joel stared at Matthias, his anger began welling up, boiling to the surface. He clenched his fists, his knuckles turning white, as all thoughts left his mind, replaced by one. *He betrayed us.*

Joel took one step forward before Matthias calmly raised a hand, saying, "Please, there is no need for, ah . . . that. It doesn't take much to discern your . . . emotional state. I empathize, I really do." Joel took another step forward, ignoring Matthias's words, his mind chaotic.

Matthias frowned, quickly adding, "What do you hope to accomplish here, Joel?"

Joel stopped, caught off guard by the question. He blinked, thinking about the question. *What am I hoping to accomplish?* He hesitantly replied, "I . . . I don't know. But . . . you lied to me. You left me there to die—you left my family there to die!" His voice rose to a shout as he stepped closer.

Matthias seemed unfazed, smoothly replying, "When did I lie to you? I told you that you would see your family at the second location—and I assume you did?"

Joel opened his mouth to respond but was unsure of what to say. Matthias nodded and quickly continued, "Yes, as I thought. Now, following that logic, if they clearly are not dead, then how do you figure that I left you to die there? I truly apologize for having to restrain you, but I doubt you would have willingly sat there. You had to have your eyes forced open for you to see."

Joel stammered, saying, "But they . . . they aren't . . ."

Matthias held up a hand, interrupting him. "Aren't what? Alive? I don't know exactly what happened last night that resulted in you being here, but I imagine that you aren't ready to accept that. When I told you that you were going to see your family, I said it genuinely, and in good faith. Now you have to decide whether or not you want to believe it."

Matthias stared at Joel intensely for a moment, rubbing his chin, before he continued, "And I suspect that you do want to believe it. So, what's stopping you?"

The rest of Joel's anger faded as Matthias spoke, replaced with sorrow and doubt. *Because if I do, Emily died for nothing.* He closed his eyes for a moment as he felt tears welling, before he quickly regained composure and quietly said, "How can I trust you after all this? After all you've done?"

Matthias regarded him with a thoughtful expression, tapping a finger on his desk. "We've already had that talk—but, I understand the problem. You can leave any past grievances or guilt behind you when you go, Joel. What happens here is irrelevant once you join them. Do you understand?"

Joel didn't respond, Matthias's words striking into his soul. *But it's not about whether or not I will carry the guilt with me—it's about honoring her now.* Joel closed his eyes, steeling himself and regaining control of his thoughts, before firmly asking, "Do you expect me to just leave here and let you blind all the people living here? You're still covering the truth—letting them think that they can survive and wait this out, despite knowing they can't."

Matthias sighed, thinking for a moment, before slowly responding, "If I'm not here, what happens to these people? Even if you judge my methods, or don't trust my intentions, what other options are there? There is no escaping the calls—in fact, if it weren't for me, I imagine that the majority of the people living here would already be gone. I am providing stable shelter, some form of leadership, and ensuring everyone is well fed and taken care of. Even if it's a false hope, what would you have me do? Tell them all that there is no 'winning,' and then leave to let them starve, kill each other, or throw themselves from the roof? Even if I am not entirely transparent with my motivations, I am doing what is best for us all, both while we are here and after we join the rest."

Joel closed his eyes, thinking. *Has all this been for nothing? How am I supposed to finish Emily's fight if she was fighting an unwinnable battle? Even though she was right about Matthias*

covering things, what if she wasn't right about . . . the rest of it?
He opened his eyes and, looking up at Matthias, asked, "What am I supposed to do?"

Matthias frowned, considering the question. "Well, why are you here? There has to be a reason why you came back instead of letting go last night."

Joel slowly sat in one of the chairs and, putting his head in his hands, whispered, "I . . . Emily died saving me. But now . . . I don't even know what she saved me from. So . . . I have to . . ." His statement drifted off as he simply shook his head and fell into silence.

Matthias clasped his hands in front of him, sighing. "I truly am sorry to hear that. While it's noble of you to let her sacrifice not be in vain, I'm not sure there is a solution to that . . . here, at least. You know there is nothing you can do here, which leaves you only one option. Leave it all behind."

Joel looked up at Matthias, a flash of anger surging through him. "You were the one who caused her to die in the first place! How can you be *sorry*?"

"I couldn't control the actions that led to her death—if it were up to me, she wouldn't have left in the first place. If it were up to me, both of you would already have let go and moved on, and everyone would be better for it—you both included."

Joel let his hands fall, his mind numb. "So what? You're telling me my only option is just to leave and . . . let go? Just forget it all and stop fighting?"

Matthias shook his head, a sympathetic look on his face. "No. I'm saying you are free to do as you want, but that is what I advise you to do; and I think that is what you want to do anyway. There is nothing left for you here—go home."

The words echoed inside Joel's head as he stared at Matthias, thinking. He slowly stood up and, turning away from Matthias, walked toward the door. As he put his hand on the knob, he paused and turned back, opening his mouth to say something but stopped himself. Matthias slowly said, "I hope you find your peace. Goodbye, Joel."

Joel didn't respond. He simply turned and opened the door to leave. The guards outside stopped him and peered into the room, raising an eyebrow at Matthias. Joel didn't hear any response, but they nodded and stepped aside, allowing Joel to pass.

He slowly walked out of the room and, turning right, down the hall toward the elevators. The guards followed behind him but allowed him to move freely. Once he reached the elevators, he pushed the button and waited. The guards walked away from him, returning to their post in the lobby, seemingly paying Joel no more mind.

The doors slowly opened, allowing Joel to enter and push the button for the bottom floor. After a quick ride down, he exited the elevator and walked toward the front doors of the building. The guards on either side wordlessly stepped aside, letting him pass. He slowly walked through the doors into the blinding afternoon sun.

"Your sister needs you, Joel. I need you." His mom's words to him echoed in his mind as he walked down the lifeless street, making his way back to his hidden motorcycle. *I have no one left, nothing to fight for—but them. I need to talk to them one more time, but not here. It's time to go home.*

CHAPTER SIXTEEN

Joel slowly wound through the cluttered streets, following the familiar roads through the city to get back onto the country roads. *I should have enough fuel left in this thing to get me back home, even if it might be close. I could try to find my car on the way out, but I might waste more time doing that than just risking having to walk the last few miles.*

As he drove and looked at the chaos around him, he became more and more disturbed as the grisly details of the sirens' effects came back into the forefront of his mind. Aside from the wreckage in the streets, nearly every building around him had shattered windows scattered across their surface. Doors were left unlocked, open, or even broken down—cars were crashed into the sides of buildings and, even though the fires had long since burned out, the blackened remains and ashes of objects were strewn among the wreckage.

Doubt began creeping into Joel's mind, each echo of

the tragedies cementing it further in his mind. Every door he passed, he could imagine a family running out into the streets, or people stuck on the outside trying to break into any shelter they could. Every lifeless car, stalled in the streets or crashed into one another—he could see the people inside, stuck outside in the chaos, unable to escape. Every broken window had someone like Kayla who jumped through it.

As Kayla crossed his mind, he felt a wave of uncertainty wash over him. He saw her throw herself from that window—and yet, that memory had slowly faded in his mind, the trauma of it diminished as he continued to see Kayla night after night. And now, he would see her again tonight—alongside Ava and his mom.

Matthias even said that he would prefer it if none of those things had happened—if all he cared about was ensuring everyone gave in as fast as possible, then he could have just not formed a community at all and left everyone to fight for themselves. So . . . maybe the tragedy and havoc of the first night were an unfortunate, unavoidable by-product of this whole thing?

As he looked at the carnage around him, he couldn't dispel either side of his doubts. He wanted to believe that it was all going to be OK, that he could stop fighting and join his family—but, at the same time, he didn't want to believe that all the sorrow around him was necessary for any of this to be true. *Or for those who died . . . I don't want to believe that they lost something by not going with them.*

He shook his head, trying to clear his thoughts. *Whatever the truth may be, it doesn't change my path forward. I just need to get out of the city, away from all this so I can think straight, and talk it over tonight with everyone. If anyone can help resolve this, it's them.*

He drove for a while, focusing only on the road ahead of him. Finally, he turned onto the main highway that led into and out of the city, out into the suburbs and eventually into the open country roads. He glanced up at the afternoon sun—though he couldn't judge the time exactly, he knew he would be able to get back to his house with a few hours to spare before sundown.

His progress slowed a fair bit on the highway, as the roads were so cluttered with wreckage that he had to carefully weave and fight for every mile. Approaching the next exit, he veered off, taking the ramp down to the feeder road. *This should be faster—at least there is a shoulder to drive on here where I can mostly avoid blockades.*

His journey out of the city and through the suburbs was entirely uninterrupted—the only sound that pierced the air was that of his own vehicle. As he looked at the empty houses and neighborhoods around him, he thought back to the house he and Emily stayed at during the first night—there had been a child's bedroom and a crib in that house. *I hope they found safety, or at least . . . are still together now.*

After some time, as he approached the edge of the suburbs, he was able to traverse the roads more easily. The density of cars lessened, allowing him to pick up some speed and try to make up for time he lost weaving through the cars earlier. Making steady progress, he soon broke out onto the open country roads.

As the miles of road disappeared beneath him, Joel thought of nothing. The barren landscape around him provided no solace, despite his preference of it over the confines of the city. The miles ticked by in silence, the environment around him unchanging except for the slowly growing shadows as the sun progressed toward the horizon.

Eventually, Joel pulled up to the small country home and, coming to a slow halt, turned off the engine. Even though it had barely been a week since the last time he was here, it felt as though an eternity had passed. *So much has happened . . . so much has changed. I'm so tired.* The gravel crunched underneath his feet as he slid off the back of the motorcycle. He looked toward the horizon, facing away from the house—it would still be at least an hour before nightfall.

Joel turned and slowly walked up the gravel driveway and onto the front porch of his house. The door was still unlocked from when he had left in a panic after hearing his mom's voicemails. Placing his hand on the knob, he slowly opened the door and entered the house. The power seemed to be out—the only light in the room was coming through the windows, bathing the living room in the golden glow of the evening sun.

Walking past the living room and into the kitchen, Joel rummaged around in the pantry for a moment, thirst gnawing at him, before finding a bottle of water. Opening it and taking a sip from it, he slowly walked back to the living room and lowered himself onto the couch.

As he sat, he felt an object next to him on the couch. Ava's plush kitten, which she had left home when she and Mom went into the city, was still lying on the couch, untouched. Joel picked it up, holding it tightly in his hands, deep in thought. The windows on the wall in front of him gave a view outside to the horizon, letting him watch the sun's progress through the sky.

Joel leaned his head back and closed his eyes, exhaling slowly. He just had to wait, now—he would be able to see his family again soon.

———

Joel watched as the sun began dipping below the horizon, each moment that passed drawing more and more light out

285

of the sky. He tapped his foot impatiently, time seeming to tick slower and slower the more anxious he was to see them all again. Finally, the last drops of sunlight disappeared below the horizon, leaving him in darkness.

Joel gritted his teeth in anticipation of the siren's initial appearance, but no sound came. He slowly relaxed, looking around the house anxiously. *Where are they?* A few moments passed before it began to get brighter in the room; moonlight streamed in through the windows, filling the space with soft, silver light. Joel felt his anxieties and fears slowly fading, replaced with a soothing calm. Finally, a smooth voice cut through the silence.

"Hello again, Joel."

Joel sighed in relief as he heard Kayla's voice, and replied, "Hello—where are you? I don't see you anywhere." As Joel said this, he peered around the empty room. He could feel Kayla's amusement in his mind as she responded.

"Harder to see me when it's not a building with glass walls, I suppose? Go to one of the windows and look closely—you'll see me."

Joel slowly stood up and did as she said, moving to the window nearest to him and watching his reflection closely. It was harder to see in the small, unclean window, but he quickly noticed a figure with long, curly hair behind him. Joel nodded, smiling.

"See? I'm still here with you. I won't be for long, though—I know a couple other people who want to talk to you, and I don't want to intrude."

Joel quickly responded, saying, "Wait, wait! Don't go—I want to talk to you about something."

Kayla nodded, giving him a sad smile. "I figured. How did today go?"

Joel frowned, sighing. "I don't know. I tried to honor Emily's memory and went to . . . confront . . . Matthias. But, I don't know if I believe in what she was fighting for anymore. I don't know what I believe at all."

Kayla tilted her head thoughtfully, asking, "Well, since you are way out here and not in the city anymore, I guess that was enough for you to be OK with leaving her fight behind?"

Joel reflected on his conversation with Matthias. No matter what, he couldn't find a reason to attempt to fight back against him, because Matthias was right—even if he disagreed with his motivations, his actions were keeping people alive and sane, even if it was just prolonging the inevitable.

"It was enough for me to leave, but I won't forget what she did for me. That's the least I can do."

Kayla nodded somberly, reaching her hand out to give Joel a sympathetic touch on the shoulder.

"And what about us? Have you thought any about whether or not you want to . . . come with us?"

Her voice was hesitant and sad, but she gave him a small smile. Joel closed his eyes and shook his head, slowly responding, "That's what I'm going to try to decide tonight. I don't know how I'm going to do that, though."

"I think you already have, but you just need to convince yourself of that."

Joel looked up, raising an eyebrow. "What do you mean?"

Kayla tilted her head and gestured around her. "You came here, away from stockpiles of food and water, and I don't think that motorcycle has enough gas left in it to get you back. I don't mean to put words in your mouth, but . . . I think if you intended on staying here, you would have prepared for that."

Joel bit his lip, conflicting thoughts rolling around his mind. He slowly shook his head and, changing the topic, said, "I appreciate you being patient and helping me, Kayla. I want to talk to my mom now, but . . . I hope I'll see you again soon."

Kayla smiled and, waving, quietly said, "I hope I'll see you too. Goodbye, Joel." Joel blinked and she was gone, leaving him alone in the reflection. He sighed, looking out at the moonlit plains, watching the rolling waves of grass.

"Hey, Joel."

His mom's voice came from the other side of the window, rather than from behind him. He looked around and, after a moment, she seemed to materialize as she stepped forward to the window, her hair glowing in the moonlight. Joel gave her a small smile and replied, "Hey. I'm sorry I didn't respond yesterday and just left. There was something I had to do before I . . . committed."

His mom nodded sympathetically and replied, "I know, it's OK. You're here now, and that's what matters. How are you feeling about it now?"

Joel thought for a moment before slowly responding, "I don't know, Mom. There's a lot of things I don't know; I was hoping you could maybe help me through that. If you're really you, I was wondering . . . Could you tell me what happened on that first night? What happened after the theater?"

She frowned, responding, "It was scary, obviously—during the first night, Ava and I hid in the back of one of the auditoriums in the theater. We made it through that night fine, but the next day when we ventured out to try to drive home, I saw the wreckage and I knew that wasn't possible. Soon after, though, we saw some people walking around on the street in a group. We went to them, and they told us a community was forming, and that they could take us to them.

So . . . we went with them. There were so many people when we got there—the building was overflowing with survivors, each one of them panicked and trying to figure out what was going on. That day, Matthias said he was moving the group to a different location—a bigger one. So, we all left with what we could carry and walked for a long time, out to the edge of the city. By the time we got there, it was almost nighttime. He led us all to that building you were in last night, with the glass walls. He had his people in each room, trying to calm people down, until the sun set—when it did, we all looked outside and saw the moon—it was so beautiful that night. Everyone crowded up to the windows to look at it. I felt so happy and blissful—I could have kept looking at it forever. I wanted to get closer to it, and I think so did everybody else— we all started leaving the building, going out into the night to look at it. Then . . . I found myself here, along with everyone else. Now, we are just trying to get the people we care about to join us too."

Unease crept up Joel's spine as she recounted the story. *That's definitely in line with what Matthias is doing, so I don't know why I expected anything else. The moon, though? I don't even know what to make of that.* Joel shook his head, dispelling the thoughts, asking, "Where are you now, then?"

She smiled as she replied, "It's hard to describe. You'll just have to see it for yourself."

Joel bit his lip, unhappy with the response. He sighed, saying, "Well . . . are you happy, wherever you are? Do you wish you hadn't gone?"

She quickly shook her head, saying, "No, I'm glad I did. All my worries, fears, anxieties, guilt—they're all gone, here. None of that matters anymore. Even though it all happened so fast and we were led out there, thinking it was something else—it's for the best that we're here now."

Joel slowly nodded, her words echoing in his head. *It's for the best . . .* Joel slowly said, "Can I see Ava, now? I want to talk to her."

His mom smiled and nodded, saying, "Of course, I'll let her know. I hope I'll see you again, soon." Before Joel could respond, she waved and walked away from the window, disappearing into the moonlight. Several moments passed in silence before a timid voice broke the air.

"Joey?"

Joel glanced around outside for a moment, not seeing anything, before something at the bottom of his vision caught his eye. He looked down, smiling as he saw Ava, barely high enough to see over the window into the room, reaching up to press her hands against the glass. Joel pressed his hand on hers through the glass, saying, "Hey! Are you doing OK? Hanging in there?"

Ava beamed at him, quietly responding, "I'm doing OK now. I miss you."

Joel smiled sadly, saying, "I miss you too, Ava. I want to go be with you, I really do."

"Mommy says you can, I think . . ." Ava paused for a moment, frowning in concentration as she tried to find the words, before smiling and continuing, "I think she said you can just come out here. Can you, please? Please?" She clasped her hands in front of her, smiling up at him as she asked.

Joel pressed his forehead against the cold glass, thinking. *There's one more thing I need to check.* He slowly responded, "I really want to, but . . . you forgot something back at home, can you remember what it was? I think you left something behind, so I can bring it to you when I come outside." He held the plushie cat beneath the window, so Ava couldn't see it.

Ava thought for a moment, frowning, before a startlingly worried look passed over her face as she frantically responded, "Kitty! I left Kitty at home! Do you have him?" Joel felt a wave of happiness and relief pass through him. *She remembers. She's still . . . her.*

Joel smiled and, holding the toy up, said, "You mean this kitty?"

Ava squealed with glee, pressing her hands against the glass. "Kitty! Can I have him?"

"You can soon. I need to do a couple things first, though, so can you go back to Mom for just a minute?"

Ava nodded, smiling. "OK. Promise you'll be out soon?"

Joel paused for a moment, looking down at Ava's eager and excited face. He slowly responded, "I promise. Go back to Mom now, I'll see you soon."

"OK, bye, Joey! Love you!"

Ava turned around and bounced away, disappearing into the moonlight. Joel stepped back from the window, feeling faint as emotions and thoughts swirled around his mind. He walked to the couch and clumsily sat down, putting his head in his hands.

The moonlight outside seemed to brighten as Joel tried to rein in his emotions. Sorrow and guilt pressed in on him, constricting his mind. *They are all . . . them. They haven't shown me anything that makes me not believe them—what option do I have other than to at least hope that they are real— that there is something better waiting for me on the other side?* Joel opened his eyes and stared out through the window in front of him. After a long pause, he closed his eyes and put his head back down as all other thoughts were replaced by a numb acceptance.

I have no reason not to go with them. If I stay, I will run out of food and water, and either die alone or give in anyway. Even though Emily died trying to save me . . . there is nothing I can do, now. Where else can I go? There is no path left to explore, nothing left to fight against. And even if there was . . . I'm so tired of fighting. I'm so tired of being alone, separated from the only people I care about. I can't carry these burdens anymore. There's nothing left for me here, and nothing to lose if I go.

Tears began running down Joel's cheeks as a lump formed in his throat and his chest began aching. *You deserve to be here, Emily, not me. You could have kept fighting for what you believed in and kept fighting for the people left here for so much longer. But . . . I can't.*

Joel slowly stood, staring at the door in front of him, his hands shaking and his breathing quick. *I can't keep fighting . . . for anything. I'm sorry, Emily.*

Joel walked forward and put his hand on the doorknob, letting out a shaky breath. After a few moments, he slowly opened the door and stepped out into the moonlight.

ACKNOWLEDGMENTS

Though I already thanked these people, I feel it should be said again that I couldn't have gotten this far without my dad, Scott, my mom, Alicia, and my brother, Ian, all three of whom supported me on this project in different ways—be it through reading and giving their thoughts on my chapters, helping with some initial editing along the way, or simply encouraging me to continue on to finish this book. The end result wouldn't be the same, and might not even exist at all, without your support.

I would also like to thank all of the fantastic people I've worked with at Scholastic to shape this book into its final form. To the editors, to the artists, and to all others involved—I appreciate your help and guidance in making this book the best version of itself that it could be, and for giving the opportunity to publish it.